he looked across at her. 'Y
he pronounced admiringly.

'At twenty-nine, I should

Which made him now th
noting, now that she could see him more clearly, that her first impression of his not having changed wasn't quite correct. The last eight years had definitely left their mark. There were lines now beside his eyes and mouth that owed nothing to laughter, a sprinkling of grey in the blue-black hair at his temples.

'Twenty-nine,' Liam repeated thoughtfully, blue eyes narrowed. 'And what have you been doing with yourself the last eight years, Laura?' he prompted hardly, his gaze moving—subconsciously, it seemed—to the ring finger on her left hand.

A finger that, although completely bare, nevertheless showed the mark of her having once worn a ring there…

'This and that,' she dismissed unhelpfully, having no intention of telling him anything about herself. 'And what about you? What have you been doing the last eight years?'

His mouth twisted. 'Obviously not writing,' he observed harshly.

'No?' Laura didn't give away, by word or facial expression, the fact that she was well aware that no new Liam O'Reilly book had appeared on the bookshelves for over eight years. 'But then, you probably didn't need to write again after the amazing success you had with *Time Bomb*,' she went on lightly.

'"Didn't need to write again!"' Liam repeated accusingly, no longer lounging back in his chair but sitting tensely forward, eyes gleaming like twin jewels, his face intensely alight with emotion.

'I meant from a monetary angle, of course,' Laura continued, still meeting the fierceness of his gaze unflinchingly.

That she had hit upon a raw nerve she didn't doubt. But she had a need to see his response to that direct hit. 'You must have made millions out of *Time Bomb*. The film rights alone—'

'And what good has all that money been to me when I haven't written a word since?' he rasped.

She shrugged. 'Presumably it's kept you in relative comfort over the last eight years—even without the drink and cigarettes!' she teased. 'You certainly seemed to be enjoying your life the last time I saw you,' she couldn't resist adding.

Which had to be an understatement! Liam had achieved a certain amount of success with the four books he'd published before the political thriller *Time Bomb*. But nothing like the explosion—and she excused the pun!—that had followed the publication of his fifth book.

Three weeks after the release of the hardback edition, *Time Bomb* had been number one in the bestseller lists. Liam had appeared on numerous television programmes, the film rights had been bought, and Liam had been whisked off to Hollywood to write the screenplay and help with the casting.

The last Laura had seen of Liam had been a photograph in the newspapers, when he'd married the beautiful blonde-haired actress who had been about to play the female lead in the film of his book.

And Laura Carter, the student Liam had been seeing before he'd left England, had been left behind and forgotten.

At first she had been bewildered by Liam's abandonment, disbelieving that she could mean so little to him when she had been slavishly devoted to him. But as the days and then weeks had passed, with no word from him, she had become angry. This had been followed by bitterness when she'd seen the photograph in the newspapers of him with his bride, and finally had come acceptance that Liam no longer considered her a part—even remotely—of his new life in America. With that acceptance had come her desire to move on, to make a success of her own life.

Her poise now, the expensive cut of her clothes, the large diamond solitaire ring she wore on her right hand, all bore testimony to the fact that she had done exactly that.

Liam's expression was bleak. 'That must have been a long time ago,' he answered her last remark sarcastically.

'Maybe it was.' Another lifetime again, she acknowledged inwardly. 'So, what's important enough now to bring you back from sunny California to a cold English winter?' she prompted with a casual change of subject.

Liam forced himself to relax with obvious effort, once again leaning back in the chair, although his eyes still gleamed fiercely blue. 'I didn't come from California,' he corrected. 'I moved back to Ireland five years ago.'

Which was probably the reason his Irish brogue sounded slightly stronger than it had eight years ago, Laura decided. She hadn't known of the move, of course, had deliberately not interested herself in any of Liam's movements after learning of his marriage.

'That must have been something of a cultural shock to your American wife,' she remarked.

'I wouldn't know,' he drawled scathingly. 'Diana divorced me seven years ago. The marriage only lasted six months, Laura,' he explained as she raised her brows questioningly. 'Because of work commitments we only spent about six weeks of that time together,' he added bitterly. 'Not my idea of a marriage!'

Liam had only been married for six months! Six months! If she had only known—

What would she have done differently if she had known? Nothing, came the flat answer. Liam had made his choices, as she had made hers. Nothing, and no one, could ever change that.

Liam gave another glance at his wristwatch. 'Look, I really do have to meet someone in a few minutes. In fact…' He glanced around the crowded lounge with narrowed eyes. 'I have to go now,' he murmured as a man who had just entered the lounge caught and held his eye. 'But I would like to see you again, Laura—'

'I don't think that's a good idea,' she cut in briskly, also glancing across the room at the man who had just entered, returning the polite inclination of his head with one of her own. 'It's been—interesting seeing you again, Liam,' she said without any trace of sincerity. 'But I have to be going myself now.' She stood up, slim and elegant in her fitted suit and blouse, the strap of her patent black leather bag thrown over her shoulder.

'Laura!' Liam grasped her arm as she would have moved smoothly past him. 'I want to see you again,' he told her determinedly.

She looked at him. 'To talk about old times, Liam?' she taunted, shaking her head. 'I don't think so, thank you.' She gave a humourless smile.

Liam's eyes narrowed to blue slits. 'I'm booked in here for another couple of days, Laura. Call me. If you don't,' he continued softly as she was about to refuse, 'I'll stay in London until I find you again,' he assured her.

At least now she knew the reason she hadn't seen him arrive at the hotel; he was actually a guest here and had probably come downstairs in the lift, which she couldn't see from here in the lounge.

But that didn't change the fact that there was an underlying threat to his words. Or that she had her own reasons for not wanting him to find her. Not yet, anyway.

'How melodramatic you've become, Liam,' she responded. 'If it's that important to you, I'll give you a ring later.' When she would make it plain to him that she had no intention of meeting him on a social level while he was in London!

He gave her an intense look before slowly releasing her arm. 'It's that important to me,' he said, with a terse nod of his head.

She raised dark, sceptical brows at the admission. 'Now, if you'll excuse me, I really do have to go.' She spoke coolly, aware of Liam's gaze on her as she walked across the lounge and out into the reception area, collecting her outdoor coat from the attendant there before stepping outside into the bitingly cold November wind.

Not that she felt the ice of that wind; the shock of seeing Liam again had completely numbed her now. Face to face with him, remembering all that had happened between them in the past, it hadn't been too difficult to keep up a veneer of cool self-possession. But now she was alone, away from the hotel, reaction had begun to set in.

Eight years ago she had dreamt of meeting Liam again, just once, if only for a few minutes. Part of her had longed to see him again; another part of her had been angry at his cruel desertion.

'Mrs Shipley.' Paul, her driver, stood by the car parked beside the pavement, the back door held open invitingly.

'Thank you,' she accepted distractedly, grateful for the warmth and privacy of the back seat of the limousine as the driver closed the door behind her.

'Back to the office, Mrs Shipley?' Paul prompted politely once he was seated behind the wheel.

'No. Yes! I—'

Get a grip, Laura, she ordered herself firmly. Okay, so she had seen Liam again. So what? No doubt he was still the charming rogue he had been eight years ago, but that didn't make her the same impressionable Laura Carter. She was Laura Shipley now; she ran her own business, owned a house in London, a villa in Majorca, travelled in chauffeur-driven cars wherever she chose to go. A single meeting with Liam O'Reilly was not going to take any of that away from her.

'Yes, Paul, back to the office.' She spoke more firmly now, relaxing back in her seat as the car moved slowly out into the flow of traffic.

There was no hurry for her to return home; Bobby wouldn't be back for another hour and a half yet. Besides, she had told Perry that she would wait at the office for his report.

She wondered how his own conversation with Liam was progressing...!

CHAPTER TWO

'AMAZING,' Perry enthused, pacing up and down the room excitedly an hour later. 'I still can't believe the way you just knew, three weeks ago, that despite the fact the author was claiming to be one Reilly O'Shea, the manuscript that landed on my desk was really by Liam O'Reilly!'

Laura sat behind her own wide, imposing desk watching her senior editor. The jacket to her suit had been discarded in the warmth of the office, her emerald silk blouse a perfect foil for her dark colouring.

The way she had just known…!

She'd read that last Liam O'Reilly novel from cover to cover. She knew every twist and turn of the writer's mind; knew every phrase and nuance, how he dotted every 'i' and crossed every 't'—of course she had recognised the manuscript that had been submitted to Shipley Publishing three weeks ago. Its sheer brilliance—brought to her attention by Perry—had been created by the same person!

She hadn't quite been able to believe it, though, had found it incredible to believe that Liam might actually be writing again. Even more astounding was that the manuscript had been submitted under a different name, even if the name Reilly O'Shea wasn't so far from Liam's own. It was because of the uncertainty surrounding that name that she had felt today's charade at the hotel necessary. It had been eight years since she last saw Liam, and he might have changed in that time—she certainly had! But if anyone could recognise Liam O'Reilly, no matter what the changes, she knew she could.

So she had deliberately arranged to be at the hotel today, strategically placed so that she might alert Perry when he arrived for his arranged meeting as to whether or not she had been correct in her assertion that the author was actually Liam O'Reilly.

It had not been part of the plan, however, for Liam to actually spot and recognise her! As it hadn't been her intention to agree to telephone him later at his hotel…!

Laura still came over hot and then cold at the memory of that unexpected meeting between the two of them. Eight years. And apart from those added tell-tale lines, a little grey in the darkness of his hair, Liam looked exactly the same. The fact that he had recognised her too—despite her own changed hairstyle and the denims and tee shirts she'd used to wear having been replaced by the classically elegant suit and blouse—had momentarily stunned her.

But only momentarily, she was relieved to recall. The self-assurance she had acquired over the last eight years had stood her in good stead, even down to the acknowledging nod of her head she had given Perry when he'd arrived in the hotel lounge.

That Perry was pleased at the way his meeting with the author had gone was obvious. He was bubbling over with excitement at the prospect of Shipley Publishing being in possession of the long-awaited new Liam O'Reilly novel. Except that Laura knew it wasn't going to be as easy as that…

She calmly brought her senior editor back to earth. 'What actually happened at the meeting, Perry?'

Perry dropped down into the chair opposite hers. Comfortably so, Laura noted abstractedly, unlike Liam earlier when he had tried to bend his long length into the chair at the hotel—Oh, bother Liam—and how he did or did not fit himself into chairs!

'Well, I covered a lot of ground with him, but we still have a long way to go, of course.' Some of Perry's excitement faded as he frowned slightly. 'The biggest obstacle we're going to face is that, despite several promptings from me about previous books and other even broader hints, the man stuck like glue to the identity of Reilly O'Shea.'

Laura nodded. 'Do you have any idea why?'

'Oh, that's easy,' Perry replied. 'It's how we're going to deal with it that's the problem. We have our hands on a Liam O'Reilly manuscript, and—'

'Can we just go back a couple of steps, Perry?' Laura interrupted slowly. 'You know why the man is determined not to admit to being Liam O'Reilly?'

Since reading the manuscript three weeks ago Laura had racked her brains as to a possible explanation for the use of a pseudonym. All to no avail. As Liam O'Reilly he could ask for, and receive, an exorbitant advance payment and subsequent royalty percentages. As a first-time author, a possible risk for any publishing house, he would receive much less. Also, a Liam O'Reilly novel was sure to receive much more publicity than that of an unknown author. And surely readership, after months, possibly years of work, was what every author wanted…?

'Of course,' the boyishly handsome Perry agreed; a little under six feet tall, blond-haired, blue-eyed, he exuded an energy that totally belied his thirty-five years.

'Then I wish you would explain it to me,' Laura encouraged lightly. 'Because I have no idea why such a successful author would want to keep his identity secret!'

'For exactly that reason.' Perry grinned. 'Years ago, with the publication of his fifth book, the man became a phenomenon. Top of the bestseller lists, both hardback and then paperback, for almost a year, the darling of the literary world, a huge feather in the cap of any society hostess.

Then the book was made into a film that carried off most of the Oscars for that year. The man was the star to outshine all stars!'

'Yes?' So far this explanation had done little other than tell her things she already knew.

'I've started with an astronomical explanation so I may as well continue.' Perry grimaced. 'You see, he wasn't a star, Laura, he was a comet. He came into our orbit, shone brightly for what was, after all, a very brief period in a single lifetime, and then disappeared again. Without trace, apparently.'

'But—'

'I have a feeling he wants to do things differently the second time around,' Perry said quietly.

'But as soon as it becomes public knowledge exactly who Reilly O'Shea is—'

'It may not come to that,' her senior editor interrupted firmly. 'Despite the fact I accept I was actually talking to Liam O'Reilly today, I had to carry out the meeting as if I were talking to Reilly O'Shea. We obviously discussed the possibility of a contract to publish the manuscript...' Perry hesitated. 'He had some quite interesting clauses of his own that he would like in any such agreement.'

Laura raised dark brows at the arrogance of the man. 'Such as?'

'No personal publicity. No public appearances. In fact his privacy completely guaranteed, or it was no deal.' Perry shrugged at her incredulous expression. 'Strange requests from a first-time author, I agree,' he commented dryly. 'But not so strange coming from a man who has already had a taste of all those things—and hated every moment of it!'

As an interested bystander in that blaze of publicity, of those personal appearances, Laura couldn't agree with

Perry's conclusion; eight years ago Liam had given the appearance of enjoying every moment of his success!

She sighed. 'As you say, we obviously have a long way to go yet. How did you leave the meeting?' she prompted interestedly.

'He's staying in London another couple of days, I said I would call him before he left. To be honest, it was one of the most difficult meetings I've ever had to attend. I loved *Time Bomb* eight years ago, but I have to say that I think *Josie's World* is even better—and all the time I was talking to Reilly—Liam—I just wanted to tell him that!' He shook his head.

'I'm glad that you didn't give in to the temptation,' Laura remarked dryly, looking at the slender gold watch on her wrist before shuffling some papers together on her desk. 'I have to go now, Perry, but we'll talk about this again first thing in the morning.' She paused. 'Although, I have to admit, I'm not sure exactly how we proceed from here.'

What troubled her the most, she had to admit, was keeping her own identity out of any future negotiations with the author. For reasons of her own, she did not want Liam to know that *she* was Shipley Publishing…!

The dark blue telephone that stood on her bedside table seemed to be glowering at her, even when she didn't actually look at it, silently reproaching her for not picking up the receiver and punching out the number of Liam's hotel.

As was her custom for the last two years, she had retired to her bedroom once dinner was over, taking a pile of work with her. She was sitting up in bed now, her narrow silk-clad shoulders surrounded by sumptuous satin cream-coloured pillows, glasses perched on the end of her nose, as she read through the latest manuscript of Shipley's most successful author.

So far, came that disquieting little voice in her head. Because she had no doubt, if they really could secure Liam's novel, that he would instantly eclipse Elizabeth Starling as Shipley's top author!

Elizabeth's latest manuscript was good, in fact it was more than good, but it didn't stand a chance of holding Laura's attention tonight.

She lay back with a sigh, removing her gold-framed glasses. She really didn't wear contact lenses, coloured or otherwise, but she did wear glasses for reading nowadays. Possibly because she did so much of it.

Not that she was complaining about her lot in life. Her marriage to Robert had been as fulfilling as it had been successful. It was because of him that she was now head of Shipley Publishing. If that position of power could also make things a little lonely at times, then it was by far outweighed by its compensations: financial security, this beautiful house in London, her villa in Majorca, the servants that ran both those homes so efficiently.

No, the reason for her restlessness tonight had nothing to do with any lack of material comfort in her own life.

Liam was expecting her to call him at his hotel. Part of her said, Forget what he expected; after the way he had treated her eight years ago he had no right to expect anything from her! But another part of her remembered his threat that if she didn't call him then he would do everything in his power to find her. And that she most certainly did not want.

Besides, she had information that Liam certainly didn't have—knew exactly the reason he was in London at the moment. Whereas he knew absolutely nothing about her life now. She wished it to remain that way.

'Mr O'Reilly's room, please,' she requested briskly, once her call was answered at the hotel.

'The line in Mr O'Reilly's suite is ringing for you now,' came back the competent reply.

A suite… Expensive in a prestigious hotel like that one. So Liam did still possess some of the wealth that had come to him years ago. She had wondered. It had never been easy to tell what his financial position might be from Liam's outward appearance; he very rarely wore anything other than denims, casual shirt and a jacket. Exactly as he had today. He—

'Yes?' came the terse reply as the receiver was picked up the other end.

'Liam,' Laura returned, forcing her tone to sound casually light. 'You asked me to call you,' she reminded him. Unnecessarily, she was sure. There had been a determination about Liam earlier today that had brooked no argument against his request.

'So I did, Laura,' he returned in that lilting voice, his initial terseness having disappeared on recognition of her voice. 'I wanted to ask you to have dinner with me.'

'I've already eaten,' she answered with inward satisfaction.

'It's only nine o'clock,' Liam protested.

'When I'm at home I always dine at seven-thirty,' she said firmly.

'And where's home, Laura?' he enquired huskily.

'Nice try, Liam.' She gave a softly confident laugh. Although her hand tightly gripping the receiver was slightly damp with tension…

'I thought so,' he came back mockingly. 'You were a little less than enthusiastic about my calling you when I mentioned it at the hotel earlier today, too,' he continued thoughtfully. 'Why the secrecy, Laura? Could it be that you don't live alone?' There was a sharp edge to his voice now.

'How clever of you to guess, Liam,' she teased. 'Although it couldn't have been that difficult. After all, it's been eight years.' And this man had been married and divorced in that time—wasn't it logical that she might have done at least one of those things too?

'You aren't wearing a wedding ring,' he bit out.

She hadn't been mistaken earlier about the reason for that glance at her left hand! 'Not all women do nowadays,' Laura rejoined.

'You would if you were my wife,' Liam rasped.

'If I were *your* wife I would also carry a certificate of insanity!' she snapped.

Then wished she hadn't. The silence that followed her outburst was icy cold, the only sound their joint breathing down the respective receivers.

Why had she said that? It was no good telling herself she had been goaded into it by Liam's arrogance. Her intention had been to keep this call as short and impersonal as possible; two minutes into the conversation she had let Liam break through her reserve.

But once again it was that cool control that came to rescue the situation, allowing her to remain silent after her outburst.

'You know, Laura—' Liam was finally the one to break that silence, speaking slowly '—you and I should have met years ago.'

'Strange, but I thought we did,' she said acidly. 'There must be something wrong with your memory, Liam,' she added with barely contained sarcasm.

'Nothing at all,' Liam drawled. 'But if you had been this Laura Carter eight years ago, perhaps things would have worked out differently between us.'

'Oh, please, Liam.' She sighed her disgust. 'It has been eight years—and in that time I've probably heard every chat-up line there is. That one ranks right down there at the bottom!' she assured him.

'It isn't a chat-up line! I'm not sure I even know any of them any more,' he said self-disgustedly. 'Unlike you, it seems, I've lived a very quiet life the last five years. Come and have a drink with me, Laura,' he pressed.

'I thought you said you didn't drink any more,' she reminded him dryly.

'I occasionally indulge in a social glass of white wine,' he corrected.

'I'm afraid I'm booked up for the next two evenings,' she refused.

It was just like Liam to assume that she could drop whatever arrangements she might have made in her social life just so that she could go and have a drink with him!

Probably because eight years ago she would have done exactly that. She had been head over heels in love with Liam then, had taken any opportunity she could to spend time with him, even to the point of letting down other friends if he'd asked to see her.

But that had been then. This was now. The two situations were completely different.

'I meant now, Laura,' Liam cut softly into her indignant thoughts.

'Now?' she repeated incredulously.

'Why not?' he pressed huskily.

'Because I'm already in bed!' she protested astoundedly.

And then wished that she hadn't. It was, after all, only ten minutes past nine!

'Alone?' Liam prompted harshly.

What on earth—! 'I would hardly be calling you if I weren't!' she answered with cold disdain.

'You might be surprised at what some women are capable of,' he rasped scathingly.

'Not this woman,' she assured him indignantly.

'So you're in bed. But alone. What's to stop you joining me for that drink?'

Having to get up. To dress. To put on make-up she had already removed. Drive over to the hotel. All just to spend time with someone she didn't want to be with!

'I don't think so, thanks,' she refused distantly. 'I did as you asked and called you. I don't think I owe our past—friendship any more than that.'

'I disagree,' Liam refuted. 'Aren't you in the least bit curious about the last eight years, Laura? I know I am.'

Laura was suddenly very tense. 'Curious about what, Liam?' she enquired guardedly.

'What's happened to you during that time,' he came back instantly. 'Because you certainly aren't the impressionable university student I knew back then!'

'Thank goodness!' she said with some relief. 'Look, Liam, I only called you at all against my better judgement—'

'Why against your better judgement, Laura? Am I so awful, so morally depraved, that you want nothing more to do with me?'

'Don't be ridiculous, Liam,' she cried. 'I don't even know you any more—'

'My point exactly,' he pounced with satisfaction.

'And I don't want to know you, either!' she concluded firmly.

'That isn't very kind, Laura.'

Kind! Had it been kind eight years ago when he'd left for Hollywood and just walked out of her life? When he hadn't even called, sent so much as a postcard? Had never even troubled himself to find out if she were okay after he'd left?

This man didn't even know the meaning of the word *kind*!

Thankfully she had found other people in her life who did...

'We have nothing to talk about, Liam,' she assured him flatly. 'Absolutely nothing in common.'

If you took away the fact that she owned a publishing house, he was an author, and it would be mutually beneficial to both of them if Shipley Publishing were to acquire Liam's latest novel...!

'We have the past—'

'It's been my experience that to indulge in reminiscences is a complete waste of time, Liam,' she told him bluntly. 'People very rarely remember the same experience in exactly the same way!'

'I remember our relationship eight years ago as something sweet and rather beautiful—'

'Oh, please spare me that, Liam,' she cut in disgustedly.

'—in *my* life,' he finished.

Maybe in retrospect that was how it now appeared to him. It was a pity he hadn't felt the same way eight years ago!

'Which just bears out my earlier statement about people acquiring differing impressions. Of the past or anything else,' she said briskly. 'I remember myself as a rather stupid twenty-one-year-old, totally infatuated with a world-famous author—an author who probably found me a complete pain in the—'

'Now you're being unkind again, Laura,' Liam cut in. 'To yourself, I mean.'

'No, just realistic,' she drawled. 'No wonder you couldn't wait to get away—from me as well as England!'

'It wasn't like that—'

'It was exactly like that, Liam,' she assured him laughingly. 'I must have been such a nuisance, following you around all those months like some faithful little lap-dog, hanging on your every word, there every time you turned around—'

'I said it wasn't like that, Laura,' he told her angrily. 'The fact that you remember it as such is a good enough reason for us to meet up for that drink!'

'You're very persistent, Liam,' she said wearily. 'Or is it just a question of my being something of a challenge now that I'm obviously not as malleable as I used to be?'

'I never thought of you as malleable!' he barked.

She sighed, wondering exactly what she should do for the best.

As Laura, there was no doubt in her mind that she didn't want to meet Liam; she still remembered all too vividly the pain she had felt after knowing him in the past. But as the owner of Shipley Publishing she knew that at some stage in the negotiations she was going to have to deal with him. Perhaps it was better to get any personal awkwardness between them out of the way before that became necessary? Although that didn't include, at this stage, telling him that she was now Laura *Shipley*...

'Or perhaps it's just that you think your husband might object to your meeting me for a drink?' Liam put in softly.

Laura stiffened resentfully. 'Let's leave my husband out of this,' she retorted. Robert, and her marriage to him, were not things she ever intended to talk about to Liam. They might have a business relationship ahead of them, but that certainly didn't involve confidences about her personal life.

'Gladly,' Liam returned shortly. 'So what's it to be, Laura? Meet me for a drink tonight? Or I come looking for you tomorrow?'

'That sounds decidedly like a threat, Liam.' It didn't just *sound* like a threat—it *was* one!

'If that's the way you care to take it,' he conceded with exasperation.

'I think I should warn you—I don't respond too well to threats,' she told him stiffly.

'Then don't take it as one,' he replied impatiently. 'My goodness, Laura, you didn't used to be this difficult!'

She had used not to be a lot of things. But it was those changes, in herself as well as her life, that now gave her the inner strength and security to accept his invitation. Liam couldn't touch her emotionally. Not any more.

'Okay, Liam, I'll meet you for that drink,' she accepted graciously.

'Why ever couldn't you have just agreed to do that ten minutes ago?' he demanded.

'I didn't want to make it that easy for you,' she told him with blunt honesty.

He sighed. 'I would take a guess that you don't intend making anything easy for me!'

She laughed softly. 'You would guess correctly. Give me forty minutes or so to dress and get over to you,' she continued briskly, throwing back the satin sheets to get out of bed.

'I'll have the champagne waiting on ice for you,' he came back huskily.

Laura stiffened. 'Let me make it clear from the onset, Liam—we do not have anything to celebrate,' she told him flatly.

'Maybe you don't—but I do.' He sounded completely unperturbed by her outburst. 'I'll tell you about it when you get here,' he promised.

Laura dressed, frowning at her reflection in the mirror as she put on her make-up. Exactly what did Liam have to celebrate? What did he intend telling her about when she got to the hotel? She couldn't believe, after the secrecy he had maintained concerning his manuscript, *Josie's World*, that he intended telling her about that.

And if he did how she would actually respond?

In the circumstances, how *could* she respond…?

CHAPTER THREE

A QUICK look around the bar and lounge area on her arrival at the hotel a short time later showed her that Liam wasn't in any of them. Which could mean only one thing…

Laura marched determinedly over to the reception desk, her eyes, with their different colours, sparkling angrily. 'Could you call Mr O'Reilly's suite, please, and tell him that Laura is waiting for him downstairs?'

'Certainly, madam.' The receptionist smiled at her before doing exactly that, putting her hand over the receiver after a minute or so's conversation with Liam. 'Mr O'Reilly would like you to join him in his suite on the third floor—'

'Could you tell Mr O'Reilly that I am waiting for him downstairs in Reception—with or without the champagne!' Laura was so angry her voice shook slightly, and her hands clenched into fists at her sides.

How dared he? How dared he assume she would go up to his suite for the agreed drink? Exactly who did he think he was? More to the point, *what* did he think she was?

The receptionist related the message, ending the call a few seconds later before smiling at Laura with vacuous politeness. 'Mr O'Reilly says he will join you here in a few minutes.'

'Thank you,' Laura accepted stiffly, before marching over to sit in one of the sumptuous armchairs that filled the reception area, glaring across at the four lifts as she waited for Liam to appear from one of them, not even sure now that she was going to stay for the proposed drink!

She sat and fumed as she waited. Liam had a nerve, just

assuming— The arrogance of him! The absolute, unmitigating gall of the man!

'I would tell you how beautiful you look when you're angry,' an amused voice remarked behind her, very close to her ear, 'but I very much doubt, in your present frame of mind, that you would appreciate the hackneyed compliment!'

Laura, having spun round angrily at the first sound of Liam's voice, found herself with her face only inches away from his own.

For the second time today, exactly where had he come from?

She had seated herself facing towards the lifts this time, and still she had missed his arrival. The man was more elusive than a taxi in the theatre district of London on a Saturday evening!

'I walked down,' he drawled as he seemed to guess some of her thoughts.

'Three floors?' she gasped disbelievingly. The Liam she'd used to know had sometimes found walking from the bedroom to the kitchen too much effort!

He grinned at her obvious scepticism. 'I've taken up hiking in the countryside since I moved back to Ireland.' His expression darkened. 'For a while it became my salvation!'

'How nice,' Laura returned insincerely, not wanting to hear the reasons why he had needed salvation. 'You decided not to bring down the champagne, I see.' She looked pointedly at his empty hands.

'It's waiting for us in the bar.' He gave a sweep of his hand in that direction.

Meaning what? Laura wondered as she stood up. That he had intended the two of them drinking in the bar the whole time? Or that he had made a hasty call down to the barman and asked him to put a second bottle of champagne on ice? Somehow Laura had an idea it was the second option!

'You think too much,' Liam teased, moving to lightly clasp her arm as they strolled through to the bar. 'You also look gorgeous,' he added admiringly.

She frowned at the compliment. She had dressed in black trousers and a fitted black leather shirt deliberately, considering them to be smart but unalluring. The last thing she wanted was for Liam to think she was out to appear attractive to him. She had obviously failed!

Laura studied him as they sipped the champagne that had been poured for them, having unemotionally noted the female interest engendered in the bar by his dark Irish good looks. Some things never changed, she acknowledged dryly; Liam always had been able to attract every woman within a ten-yard-radius, no matter what her age!

'So, Laura.' Liam looked across at her with laughing blue eyes. 'What's your conclusion?'

She inwardly stiffened at his perception, while outwardly giving every impression she was completely relaxed sitting in the armchair placed next to his. 'Concerning what?' She was deliberately unhelpful.

'Concerning any physical changes you might see in me after all these years,' he drawled unconcernedly.

Unconcernedly, Laura guessed, because he knew that none of those changes had detracted from his rugged good looks.

She shrugged. 'We're both eight years older, Liam.'

He chuckled softly. 'Very tactfully said, Laura—but in no way does it answer my question.'

She raised dark brows. 'Because, quite honestly, I don't see the point in the question, let alone the answer,' she replied tersely.

Blue eyes narrowed speculatively. 'What's he like?' he murmured slowly.

It took all of her inner control to maintain her composure. 'Who?' she finally asked stiffly.

'The man you married.'

Her gaze was cool now. 'Robert's the most kind, wonderful, considerate person I have ever known,' she answered without hesitation.

Liam looked less than pleased by her reply, scowling darkly. 'But what's he like in bed?' he probed.

Laura, in the process of sipping her champagne, almost choked over the bubbly liquid, glaring at him with icy eyes. 'How dare you?' she gasped once she could catch her breath, her hand shaking slightly as she slammed her champagne glass down on the table that stood in front of them. 'Just who do you think you are? You have absolutely no right—'

'That bad, hmm?' Liam put in consideringly, still studying her with narrowed eyes.

'What's that supposed to mean?' She glared at him, two bright red spots of angry colour in her cheeks.

'Too defensive, Laura. Too outraged. Just too everything, really,' he taunted. 'The next thing you're going to tell me is that the kindness, consideration and being wonderful far outweigh the fact that he doesn't satisfy you in bed.' He quirked mocking brows.

'You're completely wrong there, Liam,' she replied scathingly, bending to pick up her clutch bag. 'Because I have nothing further to say to you—about Robert or anything else!' She stood up, looking down at him contemptuously. 'You *have* changed in the last eight years, Liam—and certainly not for the better!'

'Oh, for goodness' sake sit down, Laura,' he said wearily. 'Okay, I was out of order making those remarks about your husband.' *Even if they are true*, his tone implied. 'I apologise, okay?' he prompted irritably as she still glared down at him.

'No, it's not okay,' she told him from between stiff lips, completely unyielding.

He sat forward, reaching out to clasp one of her hands in his. 'Did it ever occur to you that I might be feeling a little jealous?' he asked. 'After all, you used to think *I* was wonderful,' he added self-derisively.

She gave a scornful laugh. 'That was before I grew up enough to be able to pick the gold from the dross!'

Before he released her, Liam's fingers tightened briefly about hers—the only outward sign he gave that he was angered by her deliberate insult.

And it had been deliberate, she inwardly acknowledged, provoked by his insulting remarks about Robert. She wouldn't allow anyone to do that. Robert had been her salvation in a time of deep crisis.

She had also been thrown a little by Liam's suggestion that he might actually be jealous of her feelings for Robert. Until she'd realised Liam might just feel put out, the feelings of adoration she had once had for him having now passed on to Robert!

For a moment, a very brief moment, she had actually thought she might have been mistaken about how unfeeling he had been in the past. She obviously wasn't; Liam's feelings of jealousy were just as selfish as all his other emotions had always been!

She gave a humourless smile. 'I did try to warn you that this was a mistake, Liam,' she said. 'We have nothing in common now—if we ever did. Old friends meeting in this way—'

'Old lovers!' he corrected harshly, blue eyes alight with

emotion. 'Don't try to totally negate our past together, Laura.'

She felt frozen to the spot, actually able to feel the colour drain from her cheeks. Negate their past? She would like to wipe it from her memory bank altogether!

Lovers... Yes, they had been lovers. But she had been determined, these last eight years, never to think of that again. She didn't want to think about it!

'Please sit down, Laura,' Liam encouraged quietly. 'I promise I'll try not to be insulting again.'

'You'll *try*, Liam?' she repeated dryly, giving a shake of her head at his arrogance. 'You'll have to do better than that if you expect me to stay!'

He gave a rueful smile. 'You have to accept sometimes I can be insulting without meaning to be.'

Laura gave a pained wince. 'And that's the best excuse you can give for some of the things you've already said to me?'

'Without actually lying—yes!'

She sat down abruptly. 'You really are the most arrogant man I've ever had the misfortune to meet!'

He grinned, leaning forward to replenish their champagne glasses. 'Well, at least I have that distinction—the *most* arrogant man you've ever met.'

'Arrogance is not a virtue, Liam.'

'I'll try to remember that,' he said wryly. 'Now, let's drink a toast...' He held her full glass of champagne out to her before picking up his own glass.

He had hinted on the telephone that he had something to celebrate, and Laura had wondered if he might mean the prospect of publication for his new book. If it should turn out that *was* what it was, what was she going to do? To carry on pleading ignorance would be deceptive in the extreme. But to tell him the truth, after his bluntness already this evening, would be even more unacceptable…

She swallowed hard. 'A toast to what?'

'Old lovers and new friends?' he suggested.

She gave the ghost of a smile, relieved the toast hadn't been what she had expected—although the alternative hadn't been much better! 'The first I choose to forget—the second isn't very likely,' she told him honestly.

'Let's drink to us anyway,' he encouraged huskily.

'To 'us'…?

'Did you tell him about us?' Liam asked slowly, once the toast had been drunk.

She stiffened. 'Robert, you mean?' she said delaying.

'Of course I mean Robert,' he confirmed laughingly. 'Unless you've had any other husbands the last eight years? Just out of interest,' he continued lightly, 'how long ago did you marry him?'

'Robert and I were married seven and a half years ago,' she answered flatly.

'No time for any other husbands.' Liam answered his own question. 'And only a few months after I left for California,' he added pointedly.

'Nowhere near as hasty as your own marriage,' Laura returned harshly. 'You had barely arrived on the tarmac at Los Angeles airport before your own engagement, and subsequent marriage took place!'

She could still remember her feelings of absolute desolation when she had seen the speculation in the newspapers concerning his relationship with Diana Porter. That desolation had been complete when the photographs of his wedding had appeared a few weeks later. If it hadn't been for Robert—

'It looks as if neither of us were too heartbroken at our

separation,' Liam acknowledged. 'I suppose your beloved uncle approves of Robert too?'

Laura's movements were deliberate and calm as she placed her champagne glass back down on the low table in front of her. They had to be; her hand was shaking so much she was in danger of spilling the bubbly wine.

Her parents had been killed in a car crash when she was only sixteen, leaving her without any close family to speak of. It had been left to her godfather, her honorary 'uncle' and guardian, also the executor of her parents' will, to organise the continued payment of her boarding-school fees, so enabling her to stay on at school and sit her 'A' levels before going on to university.

Obviously when she'd met Liam, eight and a half a years ago she had told him about her beloved godfather in the course of their own relationship. But the two men had never met.

Obviously her godfather had expressed curiosity about this worldly-wise man in her life, and she had suggested to Liam several times that perhaps the two men should meet. It had been a suggestion he had chosen to ignore.

And the reason for his reticence had become obvious once he had gone to America and married someone else within a few months: the complication of meeting the guardian of the young student whom he had only been casually involved with for six months previously had not entered into any of his plans! That would have made everything just a little too serious—and Liam hadn't ever had any serious intentions where Laura was concerned!

She looked at him coldly now. 'I don't happen to think of any of this—any part of my life now, in fact—is your business, Liam,' she told him icily. 'Just as I have no interest in your personal life now,' she concluded contemptuously.

Liam looked completely unperturbed by her coldness. 'How about my professional one?' he teased. 'Wouldn't you like to know what—?'

'No!' she sharply cut him off before he could say something that might put her in a compromising position. Telling her that Shipley Publishing was interested in publishing his latest novel would certainly do that! 'No, Liam, I don't want to know anything about your professional life either.' She spoke more calmly. 'In fact—' she gave a glance at her wristwatch '—I really should be going now.'

'Cinderella turns into a pumpkin at the stroke of eleven?' Liam suggested.

She smiled, shaking her head. 'You obviously don't know your fairy-tales very well, Liam. Cinderella turned back into a ragged drudge. But not until midnight.'

He shrugged. 'Put my ignorance down to my deprived childhood. My mother didn't have the time to read me fairy-tales; she was too busy going out to work to keep my three sisters and myself after my father died.'

He made the remark without any show of bitterness in his tone, and yet Laura knew that it couldn't have been easy for the four children, nor their mother. Their father had been killed when Liam, the eldest child, was only seven. She couldn't imagine how Mary O'Reilly had managed during those years at all. The fact that Liam had become a successful writer by the time he was in his mid-twenties had helped all his family financially. But it couldn't take away the struggle of the children's early years.

But she didn't want to think about the hardships of Liam's fatherless childhood. The last thing she wanted was to see Liam in any sort of vulnerable light!

'Are your mother and sisters all well?' she felt compelled to enquire politely.

He smiled at the thought of his family. 'Very much so. Mama lives very comfortably in a lovely cottage on the west coast of Ireland, and all three of my sisters are happily married with children of their own. Fourteen between them, at the last count.'

Laura smiled. 'Your mother must love that.'

He grimaced. 'My mother won't be completely happy until I've provided her with a male grandchild to carry on the family name.'

Laura raised dark brows. 'Surely there must be lots of O'Reillys in Ireland?'

'To be sure there are,' Liam answered with a deliberate Irish lilt to his voice. 'But there aren't any other male members of this particular O'Reilly branch,' he explained ruefully.

'So that puts the onus on you?' she responded. 'And is a little O'Reilly, male or female, a future possibility?'

'Not this side of the next millennium!' he bit out harshly.

'Your poor mother!' Laura rebuked, standing up in preparation for leaving. 'Thank you for the champagne, Liam; I enjoyed it.'

'If not the company, hmm?' He stood up too, standing only inches away from her.

Laura wished he weren't standing quite so close. She could smell the faint elusiveness of his aftershave, feel the heat that emanated from his body. But she didn't want to be aware of him in any way.

'The company was fine too,' she said firmly. 'Enjoy the rest of your stay in London, Liam. Perhaps the two of us will meet up accidentally again one day—in another eight years or so!' She turned to leave.

'I'll walk as far as the door with you.' Liam had moved to lightly grasp her elbow as he walked confidently beside her. 'It's the least I can do as I can't actually see you home,' he elaborated at her startled glance.

Laura didn't even qualify the remark with a reply. She just wanted to get away from there, as far away from Liam as quickly as possible. If that meant suffering a few more minutes of his company, then so be it!

'This is farther than the door,' she observed, looking up pointedly at the awning over their heads as they stood outside the entrance to the hotel.

'I didn't think you would be too happy about my doing this actually inside the hotel,' Liam murmured, before his head bent and his mouth claimed hers.

The kiss was so unexpected that for a moment Laura was totally stunned. But as she felt the heated waves of compliance sweeping over her, felt her body remembering the physical joy of this man even if she chose not to, she knew she had to break away. Now!

She wrenched her mouth away from Liam's, pushing at his arms as they curved about her waist. 'That was completely uncalled-for!' she gasped as she at last managed to escape those steely bands, her breathing erratic in her agitation, a flush to her cheeks as she glared at him.

'But necessary,' Liam rasped. 'For me.' He gave a rueful shake of his head. 'I know you're a married woman, and I apologise because of that. But—you can tell him from me he's a lucky man.'

Her blue and green eyes flashed. 'I intend forgetting any of—*this*, the moment I enter the taxi,' she told him forcefully. 'You're even more despicable than I remember!'

He looked unconcerned. 'Sticks and stones,' he replied.

She would have liked to do more than break a few bones—she felt like hitting him over the head with something heavy and painful!

She hadn't lost her temper like this in eight years. If ever!

Only hours into meeting Liam again and she was a mass of seething emotions. All of which she could quite happily do without.

'One day, Liam,' she ground out between gritted teeth, 'you're going to come up against someone—a situation—you have no control over. Let me know when that day comes—I would like to sit and watch!'

He quirked dark brows. 'You never used to be vindictive, Laura.'

There were so many things she had never used to be. She couldn't even think back now, to the light-hearted, carefree young girl she had once been, without feeling a deep sorrow for the fact that she was no more. She had grown up eight years ago—overnight, it seemed—never to return.

'I'm not vindictive now, either. Just a little jaded. Now I really must be going,' she said briskly. 'It's late, and some of us have to go to work in the morning.'

Liam accompanied her to the taxi, holding the back door open for her. 'What work do you do?' he asked interestedly.

Laura looked up at him for several moments. It was on the tip of her tongue to tell him she owned and ran the Shipley Publishing house. But she knew she would be doing it for the wrong reasons, that a part of her—the part of her that was still angry at the way he had kissed her—just wanted to see the look of stunned disbelief on his face when she told him!

'I'm a book editor,' she told him economically, still clinging on to the truth as far as she dared without revealing everything. After all, it was true that she read all manuscripts due for publication by Shipley Publishing. She would be doing less than her job if she weren't completely aware of what her own company was presenting to the public.

'Really?' Liam looked impressed. 'What—?'

'It's been—interesting, Liam,' she cut in dismissively. 'But I really do have to—'

'I want to see you again, Laura,' he told her grimly.

'Impossible,' she told him firmly. 'Goodnight,' she added abruptly, before pulling the door shut in his face and leaning forward to give the driver her address as he accelerated the taxi away from the hotel.

She didn't look back. Even though a part of her knew that Liam still stood on the pavement watching the car, and her, until they turned out of sight down a side road.

Which was when Laura finally felt able to sit back in her seat and let some of the tension flow out of her.

She had known it wasn't a good idea to meet up with Liam again—had only given in because at the time she had felt it was preferable to having him seek her out. But the fact of the matter was that at some time in the near future Liam would have to know exactly who and what she was. And after spending the last hour in his company she wished she had simply waited for that to happen.

Anything would have been preferable to the last hour. To that kiss…!

She tentatively ran the tip of her tongue over the sensitivity of her lips, still able to feel the pressure of Liam's mouth there, a slight tingling sensation that seemed almost to numb her lips.

How could he still affect her in that way? After all that had happened, all the pain, the disillusionment, how could she still feel this way?

What way did she feel?

Confused. Disorientated. Angry with herself. Angry with

Liam. All of which was completely unproductive, when she needed to be focused, controlled, sure of herself.

The next time she saw Liam, she promised herself as she saw her journey was almost at an end, she would be exactly that!

The lights were on in the house when she let herself in a few minutes later and went straight to the kitchen, where she knew Amy Faulkner, her housekeeper, would be sitting drinking tea and watching television while she waited for Laura to return home.

Short, plump and homely, aged in her mid-fifties, Amy had been Robert's housekeeper for almost twenty years when he and Laura were married. The older woman had welcomed Laura into the house as if she were the daughter she'd never had, and the two of them had got on from the beginning. Laura had been more than grateful for the other woman's presence this last couple of years.

The housekeeper smiled at her warmly now as she stood up to turn down the sound on the predicted television programme. 'Had a good evening, Mrs Shipley?'

Good? That wasn't quite the way Laura would have chosen to describe it!

'It was just business, Amy,' she responded. 'How's everything been here?'

The older woman smiled. 'Wonderful. He's been fast asleep since before you went out. Not a sound out of him.'

Laura nodded distractedly. 'I think I'll just pop upstairs and check on him before going to bed myself. Thanks for taking over at such short notice this evening, Amy.' She smiled her gratitude.

'Any time, Laura. You know that,' the other woman told her gently. 'I know it can't be easy for you. And he's absolutely fine with me, you know.'

'I do know.' She squeezed Amy's arm gratefully. 'But thank you anyway.'

She made sure she was as quiet as possible going up the stairs, not wanting to wake him, moving with sure steps to the bedroom that adjoined her own.

A nightlight gave a warm glow to the room, allowing Laura to find her way without bumping into or stepping on anything to the rocking-chair that stood beside the bed.

She sat down in the rocking-chair, tears of love welling up in her eyes as she looked down at the sleeping figure in the bed.

Only his head and shoulders were actually visible above the bedcovers, the shoulders narrow, the mouth slightly open in sleep. Dark lashes fanned out over cheeks that glowed pale in the half-light, the hair dark and softly curling against the pillow.

Robert Shipley.

Junior, she inwardly added warmly. He always insisted on the 'Junior.'

But to all who loved him he was Bobby.

Seven years old. Black-haired. Blue-eyed. Mischievous. With a bright enquiring mind.

He was the absolute love of Laura's life…

He was also the reason that her private life had to be kept strictly that, where Liam O'Reilly was concerned.

Because Mary O'Reilly, Liam's mother, although in complete ignorance of the fact, already had her much-wanted grandson.

Except his name wasn't O'Reilly. And it never would be.

Even though Bobby was undoubtedly Liam O'Reilly's son…

CHAPTER FOUR

'—SAYS he wants to come in for a meeting.'

Laura stared up at Perry with unseeing eyes. She hadn't heard anything more he said since he'd come into her office a few minutes ago and actually told her that Liam had rung him this morning.

She swallowed hard. 'Sorry, Perry, what did you say?' She frowned in an effort to concentrate.

She hadn't slept well at all last night, with thoughts going round and round in her head, but none of them really going anywhere.

For over seven years, since she had decided to marry Robert, she had lived in dread of Liam somehow walking back into her life, of his taking one look at Bobby and trying to claim him for his own. Something she would never, ever allow. Liam had given up any rights to his son when he had callously walked out of her life eight years ago.

Of course there was no way he could have known she was pregnant when he left; she hadn't known it herself then. But if Liam had bothered, just once, to contact her, she could have told him the two of them were expecting a child.

Instead, she had read in the newspapers of his marriage to another woman!

Pregnant, alone, terrified, she had hated him with a vengeance, never wanted to set eyes on him ever again.

Time had dulled those feelings, of course. Not least because Robert had been a wonderful husband and father. She owed him everything that she had become.

As time had passed Liam O'Reilly had become a thing of the past, an interlude in her life she could look back at with a certain amount of embarrassment. In retrospect, she could see she had thrown herself at him, had refused to read the signs that would have told her the feelings she'd had for him weren't reciprocated.

Which didn't mean she considered Liam completely blameless in what had ultimately happened; he had done nothing to stop their relationship becoming an intimate one. And being able to look at the situation with adult eyes didn't mean she had forgiven him, or that she ever wanted to see him again either!

But there had been no way she could just ignore that manuscript when Perry had first shown it to her three weeks ago. He was her senior editor and had been presented with a brilliant manuscript, even though he hadn't known the real identity of the author then. He had brought that manuscript to Laura for her immediate attention. There had been no way, without arousing Perry's extreme curiosity, that she could have just ignored it. Even though she had guessed from the first chapter just who the author was!

'Liam O'Reilly has decided to go back to Ireland later this evening,' Perry repeated patiently. 'He wants to come in and talk about a contract before he leaves.'

'Reilly O'Shea,' she corrected lightly, giving herself necessary time to think.

Liam wanted to come here. He might ask to meet the head of Shipley Publishing!

Her.

'What did you tell him?' she asked Perry cautiously.

'That I have a really busy schedule for today, but that I'll call him back.'

Liam had decided to go back to Ireland. Why? She didn't believe for a moment that it had anything to do with their unsatisfactory meeting—from Liam's point of view, that was!—the evening before.

His reasons for leaving London earlier than expected were actually irrelevant; what was important was that his change of plans meant he wanted to come here. Today.

She drew in a sharp breath, determinedly businesslike. 'Are you and David—' her rights manager '—ready to talk contracts with him?'

Perry hesitated. 'Depends who we're talking to, doesn't it?' He frowned, shaking his head. 'This is a really tricky situation, Laura. I'm not sure that you shouldn't deal with it personally.'

That was the very last thing she wanted!

She leant back in her leather chair, every inch the businesswoman in her black trouser suit and white silk blouse. 'Power dressing' Robert had called it, but at twenty-nine, she knew she was considered very young to be the head of a publishing house, and she needed every edge she could get.

'I'm sure you're more than capable of dealing with it yourself, Perry.' She smiled at him confidently as he sat across the desk from her, playing to his ego.

Perry was an ambitious man, who enjoyed his position as senior editor at this prestigious publisher; he would not like having his capabilities questioned.

'Ordinarily, yes,' he sighed. 'But in this case I don't have the first idea how to go about it. I want this manuscript very badly, want O'Reilly's signature on a contract before he has the chance to change his mind or go to another publisher. But how am I supposed to go about that without telling the man I know exactly who he is? Worse, that I want the book published with Liam O'Reilly's name on the cover? I don't want to frighten him off.'

Her smile lacked humour this time. 'He doesn't sound the type that scares easily!'

'Nevertheless, I still think personal input from you at any meeting with him would—'

'Would give him completely the wrong impression of his own importance,' she cut in sharply. 'Perhaps the best thing would be to tell him you're too busy to see him today, after all, Perry. It is very short notice, and—'

'Laura, he's asked to take the manuscript back to Ireland with him if we haven't made him a definite offer by the end of today,' Perry put in quietly, obviously reluctantly. And with very good reason.

Even as Reilly O'Shea—especially as Reilly O'Shea!—this author was behaving with extreme arrogance. New authors could often wait months to hear back from a publisher after submitting a manuscript: the fact that they had contacted Liam—through an impersonal post office box number of course!—after only a matter of weeks should have pleased him, not given him an over-inflated opinion of his own importance! But then, no matter what the author might claim to the contrary, this *was* Liam O'Reilly they were dealing with…

'I know, I know!' Perry stood up impatiently. 'Your first instinct, as mine was, is probably to tell him to go to hell.' He paced the room. 'But I can *feel* the success of this book, Laura. I don't want to lose it,' he added heavily.

'You're sure you aren't biting off a little more than you can chew?' Than Laura could swallow. Publishing Liam's book was one thing—as long as she had as little to do with it, and him, as possible!—but having him dictate terms at this early stage of things was too much. 'He sounds as if he's going to be a difficult man to deal with.'

As she knew only too well. Just that brief hour in his company yesterday evening had shown that, if anything, Liam's arrogance had grown over the years, not diminished.

Which was a little hard to take, in this particular instance, when the man hadn't had a book published for eight years.

Except that, like Perry, she knew *Josie's World*, the whimsical story of a girl growing to maturity in a small Irish village, was so beautifully written that it was going to outsell anything they had every published before.

The problem here was that Liam knew it too!

'Difficult or not,' Perry answered grimly, 'I want that book.'

Laura spoke quickly. 'Then I suggest you discuss terms with him.'

'And if I need to talk to you?'

'Call me,' she answered abruptly. Under no circumstances was he to bring Liam anywhere near her! She glanced at her watch. 'It's ten-thirty now. Ask him to come in and see you at four o'clock.' When she would already have left her office for the day in order to collect Bobby from school.

As Amy had said last night, it wasn't easy for her juggling motherhood with being head of Shipley Publishing. But with help from people like Amy, and a very loyal and reliable level of management at Shipley Publishing, she managed to keep all those balls in the air. If her own personal life seemed to suffer because of it, then it didn't really matter; she already had more than she could ever have hoped for.

'That way you aren't going to look too compliant,' she told Perry encouragingly. 'As for the problem of who you're dealing with; I think his arrogance this morning probably answers that question for you!'

'You're right,' Perry agreed. 'Sorry.' He grimaced. 'I was just thrown there for a few minutes.' He walked purposefully to the door, obviously no longer thrown. 'I'll call him and tell him I can spare him a few minutes at four o'clock.' He paused in the open doorway. 'Wish me luck.'

She nodded, smiling—knowing he was going to need it! Liam was a force to be reckoned with—she was just relieved she wasn't the one who would have to deal with it!

'—told you, Mrs Shipley is busy and— You really can't go in there!' Ruth, her secretary, could be heard protesting agitatedly even as the office door was forcefully opened.

'No?' A sceptical Liam O'Reilly stood arrogantly in that open doorway, dark brows raised as he looked challengingly across the room at Laura as she sat behind the imposing desk in front of the window.

Laura's first thought—stupidly!—was that it was only three o'clock! The man shouldn't have arrived at Shipley Publishing for another hour!

'I'm so sorry, Mrs Shipley.' Ruth, small, plump, red-haired, very efficient at her job, looked crossly indignant at the way Liam had just trampled over her! 'This—gentleman she announced sceptically, 'asked to see you. But as he doesn't have an appointment—'

'And as I told this young—lady,' Liam bit back with the same sarcasm, 'I don't need an appointment to see you.' Again he looked at Laura with those hard, challenging blue eyes.

He most certainly did need an appointment! And if he had asked for one he most certainly wouldn't have got one. Although, in the circumstances, it was a little late in the day to be worrying about that now!

Laura slowly put the pen she had been working with down on the desk-top, ignoring Liam to smile reassuringly at her secretary. 'It's all right, Ruth,' she lied. 'Mr O'Reilly and I are—acquainted.'

Ruth gave the intruder another indignant glare before turning back to Laura. 'If you're sure…?'

She nodded. 'It's fine.'

It was far from fine!

How dared Liam just push his way in here? More to the point, how had he known she was here at all?

'Nice office,' he drawled as Ruth closed the door behind him.

It was a beautiful office; there were oak-panelled bookshelves on three of the wall's supporting copies of past and recent books published by the company. Her own desk was of the same mellowed oak and a plush fitted blue carpet covered the floor.

But, at the same time as Laura acknowledged the luxurious appointments of her office, she knew Liam was no more interested in their surroundings at the moment than she was.

What was he *doing* here?

She eyed him warily as he strode further into the room, blue denims old and faded, grey shirt beneath a loose black jacket. No wonder Ruth had tried to block his path into Laura's office; he hardly looked the part of a successful author, let alone a millionaire!

'Mrs Shipley,' he murmured, almost to himself, it seemed.

Laura stiffened. It wasn't what he had said so much as the way he had said it. Insultingly. Deliberately so, she was sure.

'Mr O'Reilly,' she returned with equal deliberation. 'Or do I mean Mr O'Shea?'

After all, if he now knew who she was, there was absolutely no longer any point in any pretence on her part concerning his own attempt at subterfuge. At least she had only lied by omission—which was no lie at all; Liam had never asked her for her married name!

Blue eyes narrowed as Liam looked her over speculatively.

Which was a little like being studied under a microscope! Laura felt as if, just by looking at her in this way, Liam was trying to discover what else it was he didn't know about her.

'If it's not too stupid a question,' she began when she couldn't stand that cold scrutiny any longer, 'how did you know where to find me?'

'I asked downstairs and was directed to the top floor,' he returned satirically.

'Very funny, Liam,' she said wearily. 'You know very well that isn't what I meant at all!'

'Isn't it?' he replied sharply. 'Tell me, Laura, have you enjoyed the little game you've been playing with me the last two days?' he rasped harshly, blue eyes dark with anger.

'Game?' she echoed dazedly, in no way recovered yet from the shock of his being here, in her office. A place he had no right to be! 'I haven't been playing any games, Liam—'

'No?' he cut in scathingly. 'Yesterday afternoon at the hotel you and Perry Webster gave no indication that the two of you knew each other, and yet you're his employer. Last night, when we met for a drink, you deliberately didn't tell me that you know exactly what I'm doing in London at the moment—'

'Not deliberately,' she interrupted firmly. 'Never that. I simply didn't see the point in—'

'"Didn't see the point"!' Liam repeated with cold fury, moving across the room with deceptively light footsteps.

'I'll tell you what the point is, Laura.' He stood just across the other side of her desk now, leaning forward menacingly as he spoke to her. 'The point is that you deliberately made a fool of me.'

'I did not!' she gasped.

'Oh, yes, Mrs Shipley,' he insisted, 'you did.'

Laura shook her head. 'I told you I was married—'

'But not who you were married to,' Liam scorned.

'What difference does it make who I was married to?' she challenged heatedly. 'I didn't see it bothering you last night when you—'

'Yes?' he taunted softly, suddenly very still. 'When I what?'

'Oh, never mind, Liam,' she dismissed, heated colour in her cheeks now. 'As I see it, you are the one who has been hiding behind another identity, not me!'

'And as I see it,' he returned forcefully, 'you've known from the beginning that I was Reilly O'Shea—and you've used that knowledge to extract a little revenge.'

'A little—!' She was so angry now she couldn't even complete her sentence. 'If you think that's true, Liam, then you must have a very low opinion of me,' she said furiously. 'And an even more inflated opinion of the role you once played in my life!'

They glared at each other wordlessly across the width of the desk for several long minutes. Laura was determined not to be the first to look away, but Liam was equally determined, apparently.

And then the atmosphere between them shifted slightly, changed, no longer charged with anger but with something else entirely.

'Do I?' he finally said.

Laura's gaze was locked with his, her breathing low and shallow. 'Do you what?' she repeated softly.

'Have an over-inflated opinion of what we once meant to each other?' he encouraged huskily.

What they once meant to each other—!

His implication was enough to break the spell. For Laura, at least. She shook her head, her expression derisive. 'I think we covered that quite well last night, Liam—I was an infatuated young student; you were an older, more worldly-wise man, flattered by—'

'I'm well aware of the fact that I am some years older than you, Laura,' he interjected, straightening away from the desk. 'I certainly don't need to keep being reminded of it!'

She was relieved he had moved his overwhelming presence away from her desk, but at the same time she was determined to put their past relationship in perspective. The way that she'd had to do for herself eight years ago, when she had thought her world was falling apart!

'You—'

'But talking of older men,' he continued hardly, blue eyes narrowed again, 'I believe Robert Shipley—'

'I told you last night. I will not discuss Robert with you. Under any circumstances,' she added tautly as Liam would have spoken, her eyes flashing a warning.

'Robert Shipley was fifty-three when you married him,' Liam continued, undaunted.

Laura half rose from her chair. 'I—'

'And fifty-eight when he died two years ago and left you as his widow and sole heir,' Liam finished softly.

Laura dropped back into the leather chair, the colour draining from her cheeks.

Every thing that Liam said was true but one.

Robert *had* been fifty-three when they'd married seven and a half years ago. And he had only been fifty-eight when he'd died five years later. Leaving her his widow.

But Liam was wrong about her being Robert's sole heir; the houses and half his fortune were hers, yes. But the other half of the money, and Shipley Publishing, she only held in trust. Robert Shipley Junior—Bobby, Liam's own son—was actually heir to all of that…

CHAPTER FIVE

'You *have* been doing your homework, haven't you?' she said calmly, determined not to show any signs of the inner panic she felt at his disclosures.

He had been doing his homework; but not well enough if he didn't know about Robert Shipley Junior…

'You still haven't told me how you came to realise I'm now Laura Shipley,' she prompted, dark brows raised over curious eyes.

Liam shrugged. 'It wasn't that difficult. The taxi you took home last night is based at the hotel. I saw the driver this morning, told him you had left something behind when you left last night, and asked him the address at which he had dropped you so that I could return it.'

Laura drew in a harsh breath. 'As easy as that?' she bit out sharply, wishing she'd had the forethought to have Paul drive her to and from the hotel last night. Except she had already dismissed him for the day when Liam had telephoned and asked to meet her…

'As easy as that.' Liam nodded his satisfaction. 'After that it was a simple matter of making a few enquiries about the occupant of a certain house in Knightsbridge.'

It gave her an uneasy feeling to know that it really had been that easy. She had thought she was safe, protected, and now she felt more than a little vulnerable.

'You can imagine my surprise when the occupant turned out to be one Laura Shipley, owner of Shipley Publishing,' Liam explained hardly.

Surprise sounded the least of his emotions!

'And here you are,' she said brightly. 'I believe you have an appointment with Perry in forty minutes or so—'

'Forget Perry,' Liam rasped. 'It's you I came here to see—'

'I'm sorry, Liam, but I'm afraid I have another appointment in twenty minutes, and as I have to drive there—'

'Cancel it,' he grated harshly.

Her eyes widened incredulously at his arrogance. 'I most certainly will not,' she replied indignantly.

Laura was due to meet Bobby from school today. She usually took him to school in the mornings, and Amy collected him in the afternoons, but on Tuesdays, Amy's day off, Laura always collected Bobby too. There was no way she would ever be late in doing that, let alone just send Paul to collect him in the car.

Although she had no intention of sharing any of that information with Liam!

Liam moved to sit down in the chair facing her desk, his long length slouched against the leather, his eyes narrowed as he studied her thoughtfully. 'You take all of this quite seriously, don't you?' he finally said. 'Shipley Publishing,' he added as she looked at him blankly.

Laura's thoughts had all been on her son, and it took a moment for her to realise exactly what Liam had said. 'Of course I take it seriously,' she snapped. 'You obviously considered this publishing house good enough for your manuscript,' she pointed out.

He looked over at her with scornful eyes. 'That was before I realised you ran it.'

She bridled at his deliberate insult. 'And what difference does that make?' she challenged.

His mouth twisted. 'A lot!'

She drew in a sharp breath. 'You've signed nothing yet,

Liam, and are under no obligation—as we aren't—to take this any further. In view of that—'

'In view of nothing, Laura,' he cut in forcefully. 'What did you think of *Josie's World*?' He watched her with narrowed eyes. 'And don't tell me you haven't read it—because I won't believe you.'

'One thing about you hasn't changed in eight years, Liam—you're just as arrogant as you ever were!' she said disgustedly.

He remained unmoved by her outburst, his face expressionless as he continued to look at her. 'Well?'

Laura sighed. 'I'm sure you're aware that *Josie's World* is a brilliantly written, wonderfully emotional book.'

'Is it?'

She looked at him sharply. For the first time since they had met again yesterday she heard a note of uncertainty in Liam's voice…

Did he really not know how good his book was?

She could see anxiety in those deep blue eyes now, tension about those sculptured lips as he waited for her answer.

Could it be, that after an absence of eight years, Liam had actually lost confidence in his ability to judge the worth of his own writing? It wasn't an inconceivable idea. It was just totally unexpected from a man with Liam's arrogance!

But she could see from the stiff set of his shoulders, the tension that emanated from him, that her answer to his question was very important to him.

Part of her, she inwardly admitted, wanted to play down the brilliance of the manuscript he had presented to them, if only to wipe some of the remaining arrogance off that handsome face. It might also make Perry's job easier later if she played down how good *Josie's World* was…

But another part of her, the entirely truthful part, couldn't do that, not even if she did feel Liam needed to be taken down a peg or two. In the face of his obvious—to her!—professional uncertainty, to negate the brilliance of his manuscript would not only be cruel in the extreme, it would be dishonest.

Liam might bring out a lot of emotions in her, but dishonesty was certainly not one of them!

'It is,' she confirmed abruptly, shifting some papers on her desk so that she didn't actually have to look at him and see the look of triumph she was sure would be on his face now. 'There's a problem with the name of the author, of course—'

'How long did it take you to realise I had written it?' Liam interrupted interestedly.

The first chapter. The first page. The first *paragraph*.

'Not long,' she responded carefully. 'Perry believes the subterfuge is because of a desire on your part not to repeat what happened eight years ago...? The excess publicity, et cetera...' She looked at him questioningly.

Liam gave a slight inclination of his head. 'You have a very bright-senior editor there, Laura,' he drawled dryly.

'I like to think so,' she agreed. 'In view of your obvious satisfaction with his capabilities, I'm sure you will have no problem dealing together—'

'Only the one,' Liam cut in softly.

Laura eyed him warily now, not liking the gentleness of that tone at all. 'Which is?'

'I—' He broke off as the telephone rang on her desk. 'You had better take that,' he advised. 'It's probably your watch-dog, Ruth, checking that I haven't strangled you!'

Laura gave him a withering glance before picking up the receiver, colour entering her cheeks as she discovered that Ruth was indeed the caller. But not to check on whether Laura had been strangled by Liam!

'I'll be right out,' she told her secretary abruptly before

ringing off, looking across at Liam as she did so. 'My car is waiting downstairs,' she informed him, standing up. 'I'm sure Ruth will be happy to provide you with a cup of coffee while you wait for your appointment with Perry at four o'clock.'

Liam also stood up, instantly dwarfing Laura. 'And I'm sure that the only thing Ruth would be happy to provide me with is the door! Besides, I have no intention of seeing Perry at four o'clock—or any other time.'

Laura's wariness returned. 'You've decided to go to another publisher?''

From Shipley Publishing's point of view, she would be very sorry if that were the case. But from a personal point of view…? She could only feel relief at having the possibility of seeing Liam on a regular basis effectively removed!

'Not at all,' he dismissed. 'I've just decided I would prefer to have you as my editor rather than Perry Webster.'

Laura stared at him with one very green eye and one very blue one. '*You*—have—decided!' she finally managed to gasp, shaking her head dazedly. 'I hate to be the one to break this to you, Liam—'

'I have the feeling you don't hate it at all,' he drawled in reply. 'But whatever it is you hate, Laura, I suggest you save it for when we meet again in the morning; you have an appointment in—ten minutes.' He adjusted the time after a quick glance at the watch on his right wrist.

She was going to be late in getting to the school if she didn't leave now!

But Liam's statement of a few minutes ago was so—so unbelievable that she felt rooted to the spot. Just who did he think he was? The obvious answer to that was Liam O'Reilly, but his name, prestigious though it might be in the literary world, did not give him the right to dictate terms to her. Least of all who his editor was going to be! If he really didn't feel he could work with Perry, then there were plenty of other editors at Shipley he could choose from—though they did not include her!

'I thought you were returning to Ireland this evening?' she queried as she picked up her shoulder-bag.

'I was,' Liam confirmed, walking over to the door with her.

'What happened to change your plans?' As if she really needed to ask that!

Since his telephone call to Perry this morning Liam had found out that *she* was Shipley Publishing—and he was enjoying playing the cat-and-mouse game with her that he had initially accused her of playing with him. Well, that stopped right now!

'Never mind,' she said suddenly. 'I really do have to go now—'

'Could you drop me off somewhere?' Liam suggested sardonically.

'No, I couldn't!' Her face was red from anger now. 'Liam—'

'In that case, before I go I'll make an appointment with Watch-dog Ruth for the two of us to meet tomorrow morning,' he told her unconcernedly.

Laura paused with her hand on the door. 'Liam, I have no intention of having a meeting with you tomorrow morning, or indeed any other time,' she said frustratedly, all the while aware of the time ticking away. 'Perry is more than capable of dealing with any queries you may have—'

'Not the ones I want answers to,' Liam put in softly.

Laura gave him another sharp look, not liking the way this unexpected meeting had gone at all. But she really did not have the time to deal with this just now; she had Bobby to think of.

'Make what appointments you like, Liam,' she advised him impatiently. 'But I will have nothing to say to you in the morning that I haven't already said.'

Liam gave her a considering look. 'Is he important to you?' he finally asked consideringly.

She gave him a startled look. If it hadn't been for the fact that she had to leave immediately she would have made sure Liam was fully aware of exactly how this situation lay! As it was... 'Who?' she prompted irritably.

He folded his arms across the width of his chest. 'The man you're going off to meet—and don't say it isn't a man,' he stated, as she would have spoken. 'I recognise that flush in your cheeks, that glow in those incredibly beautiful eyes, only too well.'

'You do?' she said sceptically.

'I most certainly do,' Liam rasped. 'You always glowed like this when you were excited or pleased about something.'

She didn't want to hear how she looked when she was excited or pleased—or to remember the occasions when Liam must have seen her in that particular state.

'Goodbye, Liam,' she told him with blazing dismissal, wrenching open the door to hurry from the office without a backward glance, giving Ruth a brief wave before she hurried out to the lift and downstairs to the waiting car.

But she couldn't bring herself to relax as Paul drove in the direction of Bobby's school, aware that she was cutting things very fine for picking her son up on time. Secure and confident as Bobby was generally, he was still only seven, and he tended to become anxious if there was no one there to meet him when the school bell rang at the end of the day.

'With a minute to spare,' Paul told her with satisfaction as he pulled the car into the school car park.

'Thanks, Paul,' Laura told him with relief, before hurrying off to Bobby's classroom.

Liam had said she looked pleased and excited, but he had obviously mistaken the reason for those emotions. She was always pleased to be with Bobby, and in his case her excitement was actually maternal pride.

She smiled with that love and pride as she watched her son through the classroom window as he packed his books away for the day. The tallest in his class, he was a very handsome little boy, dark hair curling slightly, blue eyes bright and alert, his features still showing signs of babyhood.

Liam's son…

Laura frowned as she acknowledged the likeness between father and son. It wasn't just that their colouring was the same; Bobby had a certain proud bearing in his stance, and was obviously going to be as tall as his natural father.

For the first time, as she watched her son unobserved, she pondered the question of whether or not one day—when Bobby was old enough for Liam not to be able to even attempt to have a share in his son's childhood or teenage years!—she would have to tell him about his real father.

For her own sake, she answered a definite no; after the pain of the past she couldn't contemplate sharing even Bobby's adulthood with Liam! From Bobby's point of view she was less sure. He had loved Robert as his own father, been devastated at his 'daddy's' death two years ago. But the truth of the matter was Bobby's real father was still very much alive… Was she right to deny him all knowledge of that?

Why did Liam have to come back into their lives in this way and present her with this dilemma?

'Why are you frowning, Mummy?' Bobby asked curiously at her side, having joined her without her even noticing, and with his hand now nestling comfortably in hers as he looked up at her.

She determinedly pushed away her disquieting thoughts, smiling down at her son. 'Was I, darling?' she parried, taking his school bag from him. 'I was actually just wondering if you would like to go out and have a burger for tea?'

As she had expected—and hoped!—the thought of going out for tea instead of going straight home totally diverted Bobby from the fact that she had initially looked less than happy.

She pushed thoughts of Liam away into a locked compartment in her mind. She intended keeping it that way. If she knew Liam—and she was sure she did!—then he would have made that appointment to see her in the morning; she could think about him again then.

Easier said than done! She had managed to get through tea at the burger restaurant, had bathed Bobby at home, done his homework with him, read him a story after she'd put him to bed, all without allowing a single thought of Liam to interfere. She wasn't so lucky now she was alone in her own bedroom later that evening!

Eight years ago Liam, a lecturer when he wasn't actually writing, had come to her university to give a talk on modern literature. She remembered that the hall had been packed that day, all of the students, having read at least one Liam O'Reilly book, now curious to see and listen to the man himself.

Laura hadn't heard a word he'd said!

As soon as Liam had stepped on to the podium she had been mesmerised—by the way he looked, the way he moved, the soft, lilting seduction of his voice.

The lecture had passed in a daze for Laura, and she had

still been lost in daydreams of the handsome author when she'd gone to the refectory for her lunch, picking uninterestedly at the pasta salad she hadn't remembered choosing, sipping lukewarm coffee she had forgotten to put any sugar in.

'Did you know there's a contact-lens in your tea?'

Those words! Ill-fated, if she had but known it. But at the time all she had cared about was the fact that the man she'd been daydreaming about had just spoken to her, the lilting attraction of his voice unmistakable.

Her cheeks had been fiery red as she'd looked up to see Liam O'Reilly standing beside her table with his own laden luncheon tray, and her breath had caught in her throat as she'd gazed up into the rugged handsomeness of his face.

She'd moistened suddenly dry lips. 'I don't drink tea,' she returned shyly. 'And I don't wear contact lenses either,' she added, well aware that he had to be referring to the differing colours of her eyes.

He grinned down at her. 'I know. Oh, not that you don't drink tea,' he explained as he put his tray down next to hers on the table. 'I meant the contact lenses; I couldn't help but notice the incredibly unusual beauty of your eyes at the lecture earlier.'

Those eyes widened now, even as she swallowed hard. 'You—saw me there?'

He grinned. 'Second row, third seat in. Mind if I join you?' He indicated the otherwise empty seats around the table at which she sat.

'Er—no. I mean, yes. No, of course I don't mind if you join me,' she corrected self-consciously.

All the time at the lecture, when she had been gazing at him like some besotted idiot, he had actually noticed her too! Or maybe he had noticed her *because* she'd been gazing at him like a besotted idiot...?

'I enjoyed the lecture,' she told him nervously as he lowered his lean length into the chair beside hers.

He gave her a sideways glance, a smile still playing about those sculptured lips. 'Did you?' he drawled teasingly. As if he were well aware of the fact that she hadn't heard a word he said!

'Don't look so stricken,' he advised gently as the colour first came and then as quickly receded from her face, leaving her very pale, her eyes huge pools of colour in that paleness. 'You weren't the only one who looked ready to fall asleep,' he assured her humourously. 'I'm well aware that for most of you a degree is the only goal, that a lot of the work that precedes obtaining that degree can be boring in the extreme—'

'You weren't in the least boring!' she burst out protestingly as she realised he thought that was the reason for her inattentiveness. 'I—I was fascinated,' she told him truthfully—even if that fascination hadn't exactly been with what he was saying!

'Prove it,' he invited, taking a mouthful of the chicken sandwich he had chosen for his lunch.

She swallowed hard, eyeing him warily. If he intended going through a question-and-answer session on his talk that morning she might as well own up to the truth right now; until she had chance to look at a friend's notes she wouldn't have a clue what he had actually talked about!

'Have dinner with me this evening?' he asked lightly.

Dinner…? Liam O'Reilly wanted her to have dinner with him?

She stared at him, trying to tell from his expression exactly what he meant by such an invitation. He looked back at her with questioning blue eyes—eyes that told her nothing!

Laura moistened her lips again, frowning up at him, her uncertainty mirrored on her face.

Liam chuckled softly. 'Is it such a difficult thing to decide?' he teased.

'I—er—no,' she answered hesitantly. 'I just— Why on earth would you invite me out to dinner with you?' Her frown deepened.

Dark brows rose over deep blue eyes. 'Because I've never met anyone before with such incredible, beautiful, unusual eyes,' he confessed.

Laura grimaced. 'I think you're playing with me, Mr O'Reilly,' she said heavily.

'That's your prerogative,' he conceded huskily. 'But the dinner invitation stands. And the name's Liam.'

'Laura,' she returned shortly. 'Laura Carter.'

'Well, now that we've formally introduced ourselves—would you care to have dinner with me this evening, Laura?' He quirked dark brows once more.

'Yes,' she answered quickly—before she could give herself time to think too much about it and say no!

She had no idea why he had invited her out to dinner—but she knew exactly why she wanted to accept; he was just as mesmerising on a one-to-one basis as he had been on the podium earlier. In fact—more so!

He nodded. 'And make sure you bring your appetite with you this evening; I can't abide women who pick at their food.' He looked pointedly at her almost untouched salad.

By the end of that first evening together Laura was no nearer knowing the reason for Liam's invitation than she had been when he'd made it.

They had talked about any number of things—books, art, Ireland, what Laura intended doing with her degree—always supposing she got it!—when her course finished next summer—but not by word or deed had Liam made even the remotest romantic move on her.

He had, however, asked to see her again.

And again.

In fact, within a few very short weeks Laura found herself spending most of her spare time with him, helping to type out any lectures he might have to give, often accompanying him to those lectures too, immensely proud of the fact that she was obviously with him.

Over those next few months she was to learn a lot of things Liam 'couldn't abide' about women. They included women being clingingly possessive. Women who talked too much. Women who didn't have an opinion of their own. Women without a sense of humour. Women who giggled inanely. Extrovert women. Introvert women. Women who were too fat. Women who were too thin. The list seemed endless.

By the time she had listened to all the things Liam didn't like about women, and had desperately tried to make sure she was none of those things in order that he should continue to spend time with her, Laura had had no idea who or what she was any more!

And now, with his announcement earlier today that he intended her to be the editor of his new book, Liam was obviously still trying to call all the shots!

Well, this was eight years on. And she knew exactly who she was now. She was Laura Shipley. Widow of Robert. Mother of Bobby. Trustee owner of Shipley Publishing.

One thing she most assuredly was not, and never would be, was Liam O'Reilly's editor!

CHAPTER SIX

'WHAT on earth do you think you're doing?'

Liam glanced at her over the top of the business diary he had picked up from her desk and was now looking at. 'Making sure you don't have another prior engagement to escape to this morning,' he finally drawled in satisfaction, snapping the diary shut before dropping it down.

Laura glared at him frustratedly. As he had said he would, Liam had made his appointment to see her this morning; in fact, he was her first appointment for the day. Which didn't augur too well for the rest of it!

'Satisfied?' she snapped impatiently, placing the diary neatly back in its original place.

Liam raised mocking brows. 'Hardly,' he replied, dropping down into the chair that faced hers, wearing his usual denims, shirt and a black jacket. 'Now perhaps we can continue our conversation of yesterday,' he said, looking across at her with a smile.

Not exactly. As he had said, they had last spoken yesterday; she had had over eighteen hours to recover from the shock of having him invade her office in the way that he had. She had also spoken with Perry when she'd come in the first thing this morning, knew that Liam had cancelled his meeting with him yesterday afternoon...

'I believe we concluded that particular conversation, Liam,' she came back calmly. 'In the circumstances, it was very unwise of you not to keep your appointment with Perry yesterday,' she added coolly.

Liam arched dark brows. 'That sounds suspiciously like a threat to me, Mrs Shipley,' he returned softly.

She was not in the best of humour this morning, had slept very badly after those thoughts of her early relationship with Liam eight years ago had come flooding back with such clarity. She certainly wasn't in the mood to deal with any more of Liam's games.

'Take it as you like, Liam,' she sighed. 'I told you yesterday. I run this company; I no longer have the time to be an editor too—'

'Make me the exception,' he cut in.

She looked at him incredulously; he was the very last person she would make an exception for—in anything!

She sighed, shaking her head. 'No.'

'Why not?'

'*Why not?*' she spluttered. 'It must be obvious why not!' she said exasperatedly.

'Because we were once lovers?' he mused consideringly. 'But that was years ago, Laura. A lot has happened since then. We've both been married to other people, for one thing—happily or not so happily.' He grimaced with feeling. 'Surely you aren't afraid that history might repeat itself, are you, Laura?'

'Certainly not!' she gasped indignantly. The only thing she was afraid of was that he would discover she had a son—his son!

The only thing!

He shrugged broad shoulders. 'Then where's the problem?'

'Liam, are you learning-impaired? Why do I have to keep repeating myself? I—'

'No longer edit any of the books yourself,' he finished dryly. 'I did hear that the first time you said it. As I recall, I asked you to make me the exception. Laura,' he continued smoothly as she would have spoken, 'make no mistake. I *will* go to another publisher.'

She drew in a sharp breath, having given this alternative some thought last night too—when she hadn't been remembering what it had been like between them in the beginning, eight years ago!

To pass up the chance to publish the new Liam O'Reilly book would be madness from a purely business point of view, she knew, but not to the extreme where it would damage the company. After all, they already had a number of highly successful authors.

No, it wouldn't be the end of the world if Shipley Publishing were to lose this particular novel to another publisher—it just wouldn't make sense to anyone but herself! Not that she particularly cared about that either; she was well past the stage of explaining herself to anyone.

No, it was none of that that made her hesitate in telling Liam to go ahead and find himself another publisher…

It was the wrong construction Liam had already put on her actions—that she was in some way frightened of working with him—that caused her to balk at telling him to go, and take his manuscript with him. She already knew there was no way that history would repeat itself where the two of them were concerned!

'That sounds suspiciously like a threat to *me*, Liam.' She repeated his own words of a few minutes ago.

He shrugged. 'That's probably because it is one,' he acknowledged suavely. 'Laura—' He sat forward, his expression intense as he glared at her across the width of the desk. 'I would like the two of us to work together on this. Won't you at least give it a try?' he encouraged.

When all else fails, use the charm, Laura inwardly derided. The fact that that charm had once worked on her very effectively did not mean it would do so now!

'Or is it that you don't think you're up to the job?' he added tautingly.

Her lips curved into a humourless smile—the charm hadn't lasted long! 'Nice try, Liam,' she responded. 'But I believe I have already mentioned that after I left university I became a book editor…?'

'So you did.' He nodded. 'And would that editing job have been here at Shipley Publishing?'

Laura didn't like the mildness of his tone. 'And if it was?'

'Within a few months you ended up marrying the owner of the company.'

Laura stiffened resentfully. 'I don't think I care for the implication behind your words—'

'What implication would that be?' Liam prompted, again mildly.

Her mouth tightened. 'I'm sure you're well aware of what I'm referring to. But you know nothing about my life, Liam, either now or in the past; I suggest we leave it that way.'

'I'm interested, that's all.'

She gave a short laugh. 'That interest is doing nothing to solve the immediate problem.'

'Which is…?'

She had forgotten his habit of being deliberately obtuse when it suited him. It was just as annoying now as it had been eight years ago!

'Agreement on an editor for you,' she reminded him impatiently.

'I've already told you my preference—'

'And I've already told *you* it's completely out of the question!' she interrupted briskly.

'It's stalemate, then.'

She drew in a quick breath. 'Perhaps you should take your novel to another publisher, Liam—'

'You little coward! He stood up forcefully, glaring at her with glittering blue eyes, at once dominating the office with his sheer size.

Laura stood up too, tension in every inch of her slender body. 'How dare you?' She was breathing hard in her agitation.

'How dare I?' he repeated scathingly. 'I'll tell you how I dare—'

'Laura, I— Oops!' A confused Perry stood in the doorway, grimacing his awkwardness at having apparently interrupted a heated conversation, his brief knock obviously having passed unheard between the two adversaries.

Because that was what they were, Laura inwardly acknowledged angrily. She couldn't even be in the same room with Liam without her hackles rising!

'You asked me to join you at nine-thirty,' Perry reminded her uncomfortably.

She had asked her senior editor to join them at that time because she had thought—erroneously, as it turned out!—that she and Liam might have come to some agreement about his editor by then. She had forgotten how completely unreasonable Liam could be when he wanted to be!

'Do come in, Perry,' she invited, forcing some of the tension from her body as she smiled welcomingly across the room at him.

'Do *not* come in, Perry,' Liam told the other man grimly. 'I'm sure it was very nice of Laura to invite you to join us—' he rasped his displeasure '—but the two of us haven't finished talking yet,' he added with a challenging glance in her direction.

'Oh, I think we have, Mr O'Reilly,' she told him just as

determinedly. 'More than finished,' she concluded forcefully.

Liam continued to look at her for several long seconds, and then he gave a barely perceptible shrug before turning back to the younger man. 'It appears you had better come in, after all, Perry. Although I should warn you,' he continued softly as the younger man did exactly that, closing the door behind him, 'some of what you might hear in the next few minutes may come as something of a surprise to you.'

Laura didn't miss the warning in his voice—she would be being particularly stupid if she had! Well, two could play at that game!

'I think Liam is referring to the fact that he and I knew each other several years ago,' she told Perry smoothly, indicating that he should sit down in the chair next to the one Liam had occupied until a few minutes ago. 'Perry already knows that, Liam,' she said as she resumed her own seat behind the desk. 'It was the reason I was able to recognise you at the hotel two days ago,' she reminded him.

Liam's mouth tightened at the memory of that meeting, and the construction—with hindsight—he had put on her behaviour. 'Very Sherlock Holmes,' he grated.

She held up her palms. 'Why don't you sit down again, Liam?' she invited. 'I have just finished explaining to Liam that you will make him a wonderful editor.' She smiled warmly at Perry.

'And I have just finished explaining to Laura,' Liam said forcefully, making no move to resume his own seat, 'that, wonderful as you might be—' his mouth twisted derisively as he looked at the other man '—if I decide to sign a contract for Shipley Publishing to publish my book, I have already chosen my own editor.'

Laura looked at him frustratedly. He wasn't going to budge an inch!

'You have?' Perry looked completely puzzled.

'Liam is—' Laura broke off with a frown as the telephone began to ring on her desk. She had asked Ruth to hold all her calls until after Liam had gone. Which meant that this was a call Ruth had decided couldn't wait. 'Excuse me,' she murmured, and took the call, the colour draining from her cheeks as she listened.

Bobby! Oh, dear Heaven, Bobby!

'I'll be right there,' she managed to choke, before slamming down the receiver and standing up. 'I have to go,' she told the two men distractedly, picking up her bag and hurrying over to the door.

'Laura, whatever—?'

'I can't talk to you any more just now, Liam,' she told him impatiently. 'Don't you understand? I have to go!' Her beloved Bobby was hurt, needed her! He had fallen down some stairs at school, was on his way to the hospital right now.

Steely fingers gripped her upper arm, spinning her round. 'No, I don't understand,' Liam ground out. 'What on earth is wrong?' He groaned concernedly, as his narrowed gaze took in her white face and frantic expression.

Laura shook her head. 'I don't have the time for this, Liam,' she snapped. Bobby was all that was important to her now. 'Talk to Perry or don't talk to Perry,' she added with impatient dismissal as Liam seemed about to protest again. 'Take your manuscript to another publisher if that's what you want to do.'

Liam's hand dropped away from her arm. 'You don't care either way. Is that it?' he rasped.

She glared up at him with glittering eyes. 'No, I don't care either way,' she confirmed, before turning to almost run from the room, her only thought now to get to Bobby as quickly as possible.

It had been the headmaster of Bobby's school on the telephone. Her son had fallen down some stairs, seemed to be in considerable pain, and an ambulance had been called. Laura's only concern was to get to the hospital as quickly as she could.

She arrived at the hospital at the same time as Bobby did, the teacher who had accompanied him in the ambulance at his side as he was wheeled into the Accident and Emergency Department on a trolley.

A trolley that was far too big for such a little boy, making him look younger and more defenceless than usual…

Tears filled Laura's eyes as she hurried over to him, having to blink back those tears as she saw the look of relief on Bobby's face as he saw her there, his own tears immediately starting to fall. Laura knew it wouldn't help anyone to have the two of them in floods of tears!

'I bumped my head and my knee hurts, Mommy,' Bobby sobbed into her neck as she held him close to her.

'Have you thought that there's probably a dent or two in the stairs now, too?' she attempted to tease, and was rewarded for her attempt at levity with a teary smile from her son.

'I never thought of that,' Bobby giggled, obviously less distressed now that his mummy was here.

She ruffled the dark silkiness of his hair as she smiled down at him. Bobby was so precious to her that from the time he was a baby what she had really wanted to do was gather him up in her arms, wrap him in cotton-wool and never let any harm come to him.

Robert had been the one to show her she couldn't do that, that it wouldn't be fair to Bobby to deny him all the fun and games that all little boys enjoyed.

Robert had also been the one to encourage her to go back to work once Bobby was old enough for kindergarten, and by the time Bobby had begun 'big' school, with Robert only recently dead, she had been more than grateful to have Shipley Publishing to occupy her time and thoughts.

But she did wish that Robert were at her side now, if only to help guide her through the pain of seeing their son hurt. It was at times like this that she missed Robert the most…

To Laura's relief, an X-ray on Bobby's knee showed that he hadn't actually broken anything when he fell, just badly bruised it. Another X-ray showed that his skull had sustained no fracture either. Although the bump on the head necessitated him spending the night in hospital, just in case there were any signs of concussion.

'You can stay with him, of course,' the doctor told her smilingly.

She had never intended doing anything else. Bobby was seven years old, had never spent a night away from home in his life, let alone in the awesome surroundings of a hospital ward. Of course Laura would stay with him!

'I'm just going to pop home and get us some night things,' she explained to her son shortly after helping him to drink his tea.

Bobby was well settled into his private room on the children's ward by now, the nurse having obligingly put his favourite video on the overhead television attached to the wall. It seemed as good a time as any for Laura to leave for a short time to collect the things they were going to need for their overnight stay.

'And Teddy?' he prompted, his face still pale from the shock of his fall.

The teddy bear, Bobby's usual night companion, rather tattered now, had been a gift to Laura when Robert had first visited her in the hospital after Bobby was born. It had been in his cot as a baby and continued to share his bed now that he was growing up, had become even more precious to him since Robert's death two years ago.

'And Teddy, of course,' Laura assured Bobby with a choke, once again having to blink back the tears.

Although he liked to think he was the man of the house now that his daddy was gone, Bobby was still such a baby, Laura acknowledged tearfully on her drive back to the house. Never more so that when he was hurt and helpless, as he was now. Oh, how she wished Robert were here!

But sitting in the back of a taxi, crying her eyes out because of her son's pain and the loss of her husband, was not the Laura Shipley she thought she had become, she acknowledged sadly. In fact, these moments of weakness were not a good idea, she decided, even as the tears wouldn't seem to stop flowing.

'Here you are, love.' The middle-aged taxi-driver stuck his hand through the open window between the front and back of the vehicle, holding out a tissue to her. 'Have a good blow,' he advised gently. 'You'll feel much better.'

Laura took the tissue, noisily following his advice. Goodness knew what the poor man was thinking, having just picked her up from outside the hospital!

'Thank you,' she told him gratefully, this stranger's kindness making her feel tearful all over again.

Pull yourself together, Laura, she told herself firmly as she paid off the taxi-driver outside the house, having assured the poor man that everything was fine. Bobby had had an accident, yes, but he was going to be all right. A bit battered and bruised, perhaps, but all right.

'Oh, Mrs Shipley—Laura.' A rather breathless Amy came down the hallway to greet her as she let herself into the house. 'How's Master Bobby?' She frowned her concern as she took in Laura's tear-streaked face, Laura having telephoned her from the hospital earlier and explained the situation to her.

Laura smiled reassuringly. 'Asking for Teddy.'

'Thank goodness.' Amy sighed her relief. 'Er—there's a man waiting in the sitting room to see you,' she added anxiously, obviously extremely flustered by this strange turn of events. 'I told him you were out, and that I had no idea when you would be back, but he insisted on waiting for your return. He simply wouldn't leave.' She frowned her consternation.

There was only one man that Laura knew who had that sort of arrogance—Liam O'Reilly!

'You didn't tell him where I was, did you?' she prompted sharply. She didn't want Liam even to know of Bobby's existence, let alone have the chance to start adding two and two together and come up with the correct answer!

'Certainly not,' Amy assured her indignantly. 'He says his name is Liam O'Reilly.' She confirmed Laura's suspicion. 'I don't care what his name is; the man is altogether too fond of having his own way, if you ask me.'

Even though she was less than pleased at this interruption, Laura couldn't help but smile at her housekeeper's unflattering first impression of Liam. As Laura knew only too well, Amy's second impression of him was unlikely to be any more complimentary!

'How long has he been here?' Laura kept her voice deliberately low, not wanting to let Liam know she was home just yet; she needed to tidy herself and redo her make-up before she faced Liam.

'An hour or so,' Amy frowned. 'I took him in a tray of tea about half an hour ago.' She sniffed dismissively. 'After all, he could be pocketing all the family silver in there, for all I know!'

'Highly unlikely,' Laura assured her with an affectionate smile. 'I agree with you about his arrogance, but I don't think he's a thief! I'll just go upstairs and—'

'Laura…?'

She turned at the sound of Liam's husky drawl, instantly irritated at his intrusion into the home she had shared with her husband and now shared with only Bobby, as well as at the fact that she hadn't had time to tidy herself before confronting him.

'Thanks, Amy.' She gave the housekeeper's arm a reassuring squeeze before turning back to Liam. 'I believe you wanted to see me?' she acknowledged coolly, dark brows raised.

He gave an arrogant inclination of his head, still dressed—as she was!—as he had been during their meeting this morning.

Goodness, that seemed a long time ago, Laura inwardly acknowledged. So much had happened since that time. She felt emotionally drained after the upset of Bobby's accident and the time spent at the hospital with him, trying to be cheerful when she had really felt like crying. She couldn't have felt less like talking to Liam!

'Could you bring me some coffee?' she prompted Amy gently, before preceding Liam into the sitting room.

The soft click of the latch told her he had closed the door firmly behind them.

'You look terrible.'

Laura turned again at the harshly made criticism, glaring across at Liam as he stood beside the closed door. How dared he come here, invading her home, refusing to leave, and then insult her the moment he saw her?

If he wasn't so selfish, if he hadn't been eight years ago, then he would have been sharing her distress over their son today! Instead of that, all he could do was stand there and be rude and insulting!

'Thank you for those few kind words,' she returned caustically. 'Now, what do you want?' she demanded abruptly.

He didn't answer, didn't move, just stood there looking at her, his gaze narrowed, a contemptuous twist to his lips.

Laura, her nerves already frayed to breaking point, withstood his critical gaze as best she could, knowing that the tears were still dangerously close. The last thing she wanted was to cry in front of Liam. He had no right to be here, let alone—let alone—

'He must be really something,' Liam finally said.

She swallowed hard. 'He?'

'The man you rushed off to see this morning,' he bit out contemptuously. 'The man you've apparently spent the day with.' His gaze sharpened on the paleness of her face and he took several steps towards her. 'The man who's made you cry…' he added slowly, the evidence of her recent tears obviously unmistakable now that he was standing only a couple of feet away from her. 'Laura what on earth—?'

'Ah, the coffee.' She turned gratefully as the door opened and Amy entered carrying the coffee tray, with a plate of sandwiches beside the single cup; obviously her housekeeper did not intend Liam to have the mistaken impression he was in the least welcome here! 'Thank you, Amy.' Laura smiled with gratitude, sitting down to pour the rich brew into the cup, biting gratefully into one of the chicken sandwiches as she did so.

She had been drinking coffee from a vending machine all day, had had absolutely nothing to eat, so Amy's coffee and sandwiches tasted like nectar to her. They also, thankfully, helped to eliminate her tearfulness. Having even slightly battered defences when around Liam was not a good idea!

'Now.' Laura sat back after eating the sandwich and drinking half a cup of coffee. 'You were saying?' She eyed Liam challengingly.

He gave an inclination of his head. 'I was about to ask you why you bother with a man who can reduce you to this state?' His eyes swept over her tear-stained dishevelled appearance.

She looked back at him unflinchingly, refreshed, her self-confidence back in place. 'That's easy to explain, Liam.' She smiled as she thought of her beloved son. 'I love him.'

A nerve pulsed in the hard column of his throat, the blue gaze suddenly icy. 'You thought you loved me once,' he reminded her harshly.

Her smile widened. 'As I've already told you—'

'That was before you learnt to tell the gold from the dross,' Liam finished grimly.

Her brows rose mockingly. 'My, my, you do have a good memory,' she drawled, picking up another sandwich and biting into it hungrily.

'Where you're concerned, yes!' he barked.

Laura shook her head ruefully. 'I somehow find that difficult to believe, Liam. In fact, until our encounter in the hotel a couple of days ago, I doubt you had even given me a thought for the last eight years!'

His mouth tightened at her deliberate taunt. 'You—'

'How did you conclude your meeting with Perry this morning?' she interrupted in a brisk businesslike tone; she didn't want to know whether or not Liam had ever thought of her in those eight intervening years!

His lips twisted. 'You mean, is he my editor or not?' Liam paused. 'Not,' he replied tightly at her confirming nod.

Laura gave a heavy sigh. 'I'm sorry about that,' she said with genuine regret; *Josie's World* was a wonderful book.

'But I'm sure you will have no problem finding yourself another publisher.'

'Not so fast, Laura,' Liam cut in. 'I don't want another publisher.'

'You aren't still determined to have me as your editor?' she demanded, no longer relaxed in her chair as she sat forward tensely.

'"Determined" isn't quite the word I would use,' he replied. 'It's more a case of who I feel I can work with. The relationship between an author and an editor is a very delicate one. It requires—'

'I know what it requires, Liam,' she put in. 'And we simply do not have that sort of relationship.'

'We could have.'

'No,' she bit out decisively, 'We could not. Now, if you wouldn't mind, Liam?' She gave a hurried glance at her wristwatch. 'I have to go out again.' She had told Bobby she would only be an hour or so, and it was approaching that time already.

Liam's eyes narrowed to icy slits. 'To see the same man?'

Bobby, she knew, would absolutely love that description!

'To see the same man,' she confirmed, standing up. She probably just had enough time left to freshen up and change, collect their nightclothes, before driving herself back to the hospital.

Liam's hand reaching out to grasp her arm took her totally by surprise. 'Didn't you learn your lesson with me?' he rasped.

The more Laura tried to twist her arm out of his grasp, the tighter his hold became. She was breathing hard with agitation when she finally looked up at him. 'Which lesson would that be, Liam?' she challenged, head thrown back as she looked at him contemptuously. 'How to tell the bastards from the good guys?'

Blue eyes seemed to catch fire as he glared down at her, the fierceness of that gaze finally settling on her slightly parted lips. 'You'll never know how hard I tried to be a good guy with you, Laura,' he muttered.

Her mouth turned down scornfully. 'You didn't try hard enough! Now, let me go!' Once again she tired to wrench her arm out of his grasp.

'I let you go once before, and lived to regret it,' he murmured grimly, shaking his head. 'If you think I'm going to do it now, when there's nothing and no one standing between us, then you're out of your mind!'

Laura stopped struggling to stare up at him, hardly breathing, very aware of the close proximity of their two bodies, suddenly feeling incredibly hot.

He was so close now she could see every pore of his skin, the dark shadow of stubble on his chin that indicated he was in need of his second shave of the day, the grim lines beside his mouth and eyes, those eyes so deeply blue it was impossible to see where the iris ended and the pupil began.

She felt the wanton weakness of her body as Liam slowly, determinedly, began to draw her up against him, those firmly sculptured lips almost touching hers now, their breath intermingled.

'No!' She pulled back so sharply she took Liam completely by surprise, releasing herself from his grasp but knowing she would have bruises on her wrist later because of her abrupt action.

Bruises? They were nothing compared to the other damage Liam could wreak in her life if he got too close!

Because Liam was wrong when he said no one stood

between them. Bobby stood between them. And he always would.

But she acknowledged it wasn't only Bobby that had prevented her from giving in to that momentary weakness she had felt towards Liam. Her own pride wouldn't allow him to see that he could still affect her in this way!

Her eyes sparkled with anger as she glared across at him. 'I would like you to leave, Liam,' she bit out tautly. 'Now!' she added viciously, as he would have spoken. 'You weren't invited here, have no right to be here.' She shook her head. 'And now I would like you to leave!'

A nerve pulsed in his tightly clenched jaw as he continued to look at her for long, breathless seconds. Finally, he gave a harshly controlled sigh. 'All right, Laura, I'll go,' he told her. 'But I'm not leaving London.'

She drew in a sharp breath, reaction starting to set in as she began to tremble. 'That is completely—'

'Or you,' Liam added huskily.

Her head went back proudly, her smile scornful. 'That presupposes I want you to stay, Liam—and I'm sure I've made it more than obvious that's the last thing I want!'

His mouth twisted into a rueful smile. 'What you want and what you get are often two completely different things.'

'You already taught me that particular lesson eight years ago,' she flew back at him.

His expression softened. 'I never meant to hurt you, Laura—'

'Who knows—or cares—what you meant to do, Liam?' she cut in hotly. 'The result was the same! Now, will you please go?'

'I will.' He nodded. 'But you haven't seen the last of me,' he promised, his Irish brogue very much in evidence.

And he let himself out of the sitting-room and then out of the house…!

Laura sat down—before her legs gave way beneath her. She was shaking so badly by this time that it was a distinct possibility that was what would happen!

What was she going to do?

She knew from what he had said that Liam had no intention of disappearing from her life in the near future, obviously finding this more mature and self-confident Laura much more interesting than he had found the totally besotted Laura eight years ago.

Well, she had no intention of letting him anywhere near the life she had now. She would instruct Amy never to let him in the house again, would leave the same instructions with the reception at Shipley Publishing. The way her life was now, with very little other than Bobby and the office to occupy her time, that should at least make things a little more difficult for him to get to her again.

Although, knowing Liam as she did, she had a feeling he would find a way round that if he felt determined enough…

CHAPTER SEVEN

SHE spent a very restless night at the hospital with Bobby. The unfamiliar surroundings meant he didn't sleep very well and, consequently, neither did she. Hospitals were amazingly noisy places, she decided, and with the nurse checking Bobby's observations every two hours they weren't exactly restful either!

The two of them were rather relieved the following morning when the consultant decided Bobby could go home, that his bruised head and knee could be better dealt with there.

In fact, Bobby went straight back to bed for a long sleep as soon as they reached the house, leaving Laura, with Amy to keep an eye on the sleeping Bobby, to check in at the office.

'Oh, and a Janey Wilson from the *National Daily* has rung three times already this morning,' Ruth informed her, once the immediate mail had been dealt with. 'She wouldn't say what it was about, but asked if you could call her back if you came in to the office today.' She handed Laura a slip of paper with the reporter's telephone number on before returning to her own adjoining office.

Laura looked down at the telephone number. She wasn't familiar with the reporter, although the newspaper she worked for was known for its sensationalism. What on earth could Janey Wilson want to talk to her about?

'I'm interested to know if you have any comment to make about the rumour that you're going to publish the new, long-awaited Liam O'Reilly novel?' The female reporter came straight to the point when Laura returned her calls.

Laura's hands began to shake. Rumour? Started by whom?

'Mrs Shipley?' Janey Wilson prompted sharply at her continued silence.

She had been completely thrown by this woman's opening question, and her stunned silence would not have helped the situation!

'I have no idea where you came by such information, Miss Wilson,' she finally came back smoothly, 'but—'

'My source is extremely reliable, I can assure you,' the other woman put in determinedly.

How reliable? Who could it be? More to the point, what was Liam going to say, after his forceful comments concerning no publicity, about this breach of confidence?

'I'm sure you believe that it is,' Laura dismissed lightly. 'But I have to inform you that we have no plans—immediate or otherwise—to publish a Liam O'Reilly novel. Always supposing he's actually written one,' she added brightly.

All the time her thoughts were racing! Liam was going to be absolutely furious if it became public knowledge that he had written a new novel. It didn't take too much intelligence to know who he was going to blame for this security breach.

Ruth, as her secretary, knew that Liam had been to her office, but would have had no idea why. Which left only Perry and herself aware that the manuscript they had received almost a month ago was in reality a Liam O'Reilly novel.

Well, she knew for certain that *she* wasn't this woman's extremely reliable, source, which only left Perry. Could Perry have—? She knew he was ambitious, that he wanted this Liam O'Reilly novel badly, but there was no way Laura could believe her senior editor would have stooped to such a level to achieve it. Besides, making the novel public was likely to have the opposite effect; Liam would simply take his manuscript and disappear back to Ireland with it!

'My source also tells me that you are actually going to be Mr O'Reilly's editor.' Janey Wilson softly interrupted her thoughts.

Laura drew in a sharp breath. 'That is a very definite lie,' she refuted.

'Do I have your permission to quote you on both those comments?' the reporter came back eagerly.

Did she? At the moment, not having had time to speak to Perry yet today, Laura had no idea whether or not they even still had Liam's manuscript on the premises!

'You have my permission to quote me as saying no comment to both those questions,' Laura came back cagily. The newspaper this woman worked for might deal in sensationalism, but there was no way Laura was actually going to contribute to it!

'Interesting,' the reporter drawled thoughtfully, in a way that Laura definitely wasn't happy with! But what else could she have said? She really didn't have any idea whether or not they still had Liam's manuscript.

'"No comment" will do just fine,' Janey Wilson told her politely. 'And thanks for taking the time to return my calls.' The reporter rang off.

If Laura had known what those calls were about—!

She slowly replaced her own receiver, wondering what she should do next. Much as she didn't relish the idea, she knew she would have to warn Liam of the reporter's interest. Because if Janey Wilson managed to track him down to the hotel, bombarding him with questions about his new novel, Laura had no doubt whose blood Liam would be after!

But before she committed herself to talking to Liam again she decided to check with Perry. The completely blank look on her senior editor's face when she told him of the reporter's interest was answer enough; Perry wasn't Janey Wilson's source either.

Laura frowned. 'Do we still have the manuscript of *Josie's World*?'

Perry gave a smile. 'Well, O'Reilly hasn't demanded it back yet, if that's what you mean.'

That was exactly what she meant. Although after Liam's statement yesterday—that he hadn't given up on the idea of having her as his editor—amongst other things!—she had somehow thought Shipley Publishing would still be in possession of the manuscript.

Her mouth quirked without humour. 'After that telephone call from Janey Wilson it can only be a matter of time, I'm afraid.' She grimaced, standing up to leave. 'I'm sorry, Perry. I know how much you wanted that manuscript.'

Even if she hadn't.

And still didn't.

But neither did she relish the idea of telling Liam of a reporter's interest in the novel he was ambiguous about—to say the least!

However, as there was no one else who could tell him, she had little choice in the matter!

Not that that made her feel any better as she waited in the lounge of his hotel for Liam to come down from his suite and join her.

She'd had Paul drive her here on her way home. She'd arrived a few minutes ago, ordering a pot of coffee for two to steady her nerves before asking the receptionist to call

Liam's suite and tell him she was waiting downstairs to see him. She had no doubt that it would be far from a pleasant meeting.

If any meeting with Liam could be called pleasant nowadays!

'Well, this is a surprise!' Liam drawled as he appeared in front of her.

Laura hadn't even bothered to look at the lift or the stairs as she waited for him this time; this man's appearances were just mysterious!

She swallowed hard as she looked up at him. 'Would you like to join me for coffee?' She indicated the second cup on the tray.

Dark brows rose over those mocking blue eyes. 'An even nicer surprise,' Liam murmured as he sat down in the chair next to hers, not having bothered to put on a jacket, today wearing black denims and a black shirt.

Appropriate colours? Laura grimaced inwardly.

'You remembered,' he said appreciatively. 'How I like my coffee,' he explained at her questioning glance, taking the cup of coffee she had just poured for him.

Black, with no sugar. Not such a big thing for her to have remembered. And yet she was irritated with herself for having done so; she had tried so hard the last eight years to forget everything about him!

She shrugged. 'I thought you could add your own cream and sugar if you wanted them.'

Amusement darkened his eyes now. 'Did you?' he said, sipping the black unsweetened brew. 'It's good to see you, Laura, but I had the distinct impression, when we parted yesterday, that you had no wish to ever see me again,' he remarked conversationally.

Laura felt her stomach perform a distinct somersault and wished herself far away from here. And Liam!

She moistened dry lips. 'Circumstances change.'

'They certainly do.' He nodded with a grin, obviously enjoying himself.

At her expense! Oh, how she wished she could wipe that self-satisfied smile off his face. Well...she could. But the method of achieving it wasn't guaranteed to let her escape without feeling the razor-edge of Liam's anger.

'There's something I need to discuss with you, Liam,' she began determinedly.

He relaxed back in his chair, feet crossed at his ankles. 'Discuss away,' he invited.

'I—it's a little difficult to know where to start,' she said awkwardly, not relishing the anger that she knew was to come.

'The beginning is always a good place,' he observed.

Her eyes flashed with sparkling colour as she glared at him. 'Very funny,' she snapped. 'In this case I have no idea where the beginning is. You see—'

'Did you have a good time last night?' Liam cut in abruptly, eyes suddenly narrowed with speculation.

'A good—? Liam, I didn't come here to discuss my private life,' she stated irritatedly, all the more impatient because she felt at a disadvantage in this particular situation.

'A few of the social niceties between us might not come amiss.' He shrugged broad shoulders.

'I don't have the time for social niceties—'

'In a hurry again, are you?' he asked speculatively, blue gaze narrowed. 'Your relationship might benefit from keeping him waiting once in a while.'

So they were back to that imaginary man in her life. 'Liam, I've come here to discuss business—'

'I thought you had decided not to publish my book?' He raised dark brows.

'I have never said that,' she replied tersely. 'Only that your choice of editor is unacceptable.'

'Still feel the same way?'

After she had finished telling him about the reporter's interest in his novel Laura didn't think it would matter much to Liam *how* she felt!

'I'm sure we could work something out...' she began cautiously.

'You *have* changed your mind,' he pounced triumphantly. 'I—'

'Liam, you're going way too fast,' Laura interrupted him. 'I said we *could* have worked something out, not that we are! You see...' She moistened dry lips, not quite able to meet his eyes now. 'There's been a development—and I want you to be aware from the onset that I do not hold any employee of Shipley Publishing responsible—'

'Liam! What luck! Sorry for interrupting.' The young woman who had arrived unexpectedly beside them turned to give Laura an apologetic smile. 'I just need a few words with Liam, and then I'll leave the two of you in peace.' She turned back to Liam. 'I thought you would like to know that—'

'Would you excuse us for a few minutes, Laura?' Liam stood up, his expression grim as he took a firm hold of the other woman's arm. 'This is private, I'm afraid.'

It always had been when a pretty woman was involved. And the newcomer was definitely that: tall and long-legged, in denims and a sweatshirt, a mane of curling blonde hair cascading down her back, beautiful face bare of make-up. Liam obviously hadn't lost his touch where beautiful women were concerned!

'Please, go ahead,' Laura invited, turning her interest to pouring herself another cup of coffee.

But that didn't mean she wasn't completely aware of

Liam and the beautiful blonde as they moved out into the reception area, their conversation quietly intense. Although the other woman—probably aged in her late twenties, like Laura—didn't look particularly concerned at having found Liam drinking coffee with another woman.

Probably because she knew she didn't have anything to fear from her, Laura acknowledged heavily. If things had been different, if she hadn't so much to lose by letting Liam too close to her now, she might possibly have allowed herself the indulgence of the brief relationship with him that he seemed to want—if only to finally rid herself of the ghost of the past!

But, as it was, there were too many things about her that Liam didn't know—must never know. So, even to a complete stranger, like the beautiful blonde Liam was talking to, it must be obvious that Laura's body language was all wrong for there to be any intimacy between herself and Liam.

Laura was unable to resist looking across at the other couple from beneath lowered dark lashes, analysing their own body language. Friendly, she would guess, but not intimate. Not yet, anyway!

The beautiful blonde was glancing across at Laura too now, as she continued to talk to Liam. Laura instantly turned away. But that didn't stop her wondering exactly what explanation Liam was giving the other woman for finding him here with her. Knowing Liam, it would sound plausible, whatever it was!

Laura turned back just in time to see the blonde woman reach up to kiss one of Liam's cheeks, then raising a hand in parting to Laura as she turned and hurried towards the hotel exit.

'Sorry about that,' Liam said as he rejoined Laura in the

lounge. 'An old friend just wanting to say hello,' he added as he dropped back into the chair beside hers.

A 'hello' he definitely hadn't wanted Laura to witness too closely!

'Really?' Laura murmured dryly.

'Really,' he echoed. 'I was at university with her brother.'

How nice for him that his university friends had such beautiful sisters!

Bitch, bitchy, Laura instantly rebuked herself. Liam had always liked beautiful women. Besides, it was none of her business.

'You were saying…?' Liam prompted, obviously also of the opinion that the sister of his old university friend was not Laura's business.

And compared with what Laura had to tell him now—albeit reluctantly—he was right!

'I may just as well come straight out with it,' she said flatly. 'You're going to be furious no matter how nicely I try to break the news to you!'

Dark brows rose over mocking blue eyes. 'I am?'

'Undoubtedly,' Laura sighed. 'Although I do reiterate, none of my employees is responsible for what I'm about to tell you.' She looked at him challengingly.

'I believe you,' Liam replied, holding up defensive hands. 'If I'm ever in a fight, Laura, I hope I have you on my side; at the moment you look like a lioness defending her cubs!'

Probably because she felt like one! She was also using the tactic, she acknowledged ruefully, that attack was better than defence!

'Very well.' She nodded. 'I received a telephone call from a reporter earlier today. She wanted confirmation that

Shipley Publishing is to print the next Liam O'Reilly novel, with me as your editor!' There, she had said it!

Light the blue touch-paper and stand well back. She inwardly grimaced.

Except nothing happened!

The blue touch-paper had definitely been lit, was probably still smouldering inside, but outwardly there was no sign of it…!

Liam continued to look at her with narrowed eyes, a nerve pulsing in his cheek, his mouth grim, his eyes unfathomable.

As with a smouldering but unexploded firework, Laura was left with a question: did she go and check that it was alight, or did she continue to stand well back in case the explosion was only delayed?

She didn't know!

Her nervousness only increased as the seconds ticked by with no reaction from Liam. Why didn't he say something? Anything!

Finally she could stand the suspense no longer. 'Liam—'

'And what—' Liam's voice was icily controlled '—did you reply to such an enquiry?'

She gritted her teeth. 'No comment.'

That silence again. She couldn't bear it. Why didn't he just scream and shout, demand an explanation? Which she didn't have!

'Well, that's…unoriginal, if nothing else,' he finally drawled sarcastically.

'What would you have had me say?' Laura countered, stung into being defensive after all. 'You have to agree this situation is unusual—to say the least. Subterfuge just isn't my style!'

'Implying that it's mine?' Liam prompted mildly.

Angry colour darkened her cheeks. 'You're the one insisting on secrecy!'

'Then it appears I've been wasting my time, doesn't it?' he replied. 'What are you going to do about it?'

'Me?' she responded. 'What can I do about it?'

'Well, for one thing, you could stop being so stubborn about agreeing to publish my book!'

It wasn't just a book, and they both knew it. It was an assured bestseller. 'And the second thing?'

'Well, as we seem to have been presented with a *fait accompli*, why don't you stop being so difficult about acting as my editor, too?'

There was something very wrong with this conversation, something that didn't add up. What? Ah, she had it. Why *wasn't* Liam screaming and shouting, demanding an explanation…? After being absolutely adamant concerning the need for secrecy concerning his novel, he would be perfectly within his rights to be blazingly angry. And yet he wasn't…

Three people knew about Liam's book: herself, Perry, and Liam himself. She had already eliminated the first two—which only left Liam…!

No, Liam couldn't have given that information to a reporter himself! It didn't make sense—

Why didn't it? A *fait accompli*, he had just said. And she was the one, not Liam, who had been presented with it…

But why?

It just didn't make any sense. She had to be wrong. Liam—

'What are you thinking?' He watched her with narrowed eyes.

Nonsense. Utter nonsense. There was absolutely no reason why Liam should have leaked the information to the

press about his book himself. It went against everything he had previously told her he wanted concerning the publication of *Josie's World.*

'It isn't important.' She shook her head dismissively. 'So, you're saying you would still like Shipley to publish your novel?'

Liam shrugged. 'I never had a problem with it. Only with your choice of editor,' he added pointedly.

'And the publicity this reporter's article may incur?'

He shrugged again. 'I'm sure you're more than capable of dealing with it.'

'I may be,' she conceded. 'But what about you? It's the one thing you've maintained you definitely don't want.'

'I still don't,' he agreed. 'But if it's handled properly—' he gave her a sharp look '—the whole thing will just become a nine-day wonder. It may resurface once the book is published—'

'There's no may about it,' Laura warned him determinedly.

'Hopefully by that time I shall be safely back in Ireland, my whereabouts unknown by anyone except my lawyer,' he confirmed pointedly.

Because their only address for him was that post office box in London…

Laura gave him a narrow-eyed look, still not convinced. 'I must say,' she said slowly, 'you're taking all of this much more calmly than I expected.'

Liam grinned. 'I am, aren't I?' he agreed.

Laura's earlier suspicions weren't in any way lessened by this reply. If Liam had decided that publicity wouldn't hurt him after all, despite what he had earlier maintained to the contrary, then there was absolutely no reason why he couldn't have been the one to leak the information to the press. And neatly present her with that *fait accompli.*

It did seem a little extreme just as a means of achieving his own way. But, in a warped sort of way, it also made sense. Much more sense than the information having been leaked from anyone at Shipley Publishing.

And what more extremely reliable source could there be than the author himself…?

Laura sat back in her chair, looking across at Liam with narrowed eyes. Would he really have gone to that extreme just to ensure he got his own way—having her as his editor?

It seemed unbelievable, and yet…

'What is it?' he demanded, watching her closely.

Laura had been aware of that scrutiny, but her thoughts remained her own. 'I'm not sure,' she answered softly. 'Tell me, Liam, the young lady who was just here—'

'I told you, she's the sister of an old university friend,' he cut in harshly.

Laura nodded. 'And her name would be…?'

Liam was scowling now, sitting tensely forward on his own chair. 'What does her name have to do with anything?' he rasped.

She wasn't sure. Yet. But Liam had made no attempt to introduce the two women earlier; in fact he had seemed anxious to keep them apart. Which had been extremely rude of him. Although perhaps understandable if the other woman were a current romantic involvement in his life. But it might have another explanation…

Also, though she could be imagining it, now that Laura thought about it, the leggy blonde's voice had sounded vaguely familiar…

Laura drew in a sharp breath. 'Her name wouldn't happen to be Wilson, would it? Janey Wilson? As in Janey Wilson, reporter for the *National Daily*?'

She watched Liam closely for his reaction to her suggestion noting the way the pupils of his eyes widened and then contracted, the slight increase in grimness about his mouth, the nerve pulsing in his throat.

Her mouth quirked disgustedly. 'I can see that it is,' she bit out, shaking her head. 'Why, Liam?' She frowned.

But she already knew the answer to that. Liam was determined to have his own way concerning his publisher and editor, and had decided, after meeting her again, that she was to be both those things. He was even willing to sacrifice his own privacy to achieve that objective—had hoped to use Janey Wilson's newspaper article as a means of pressurising Laura into accepting those conditions.

'Don't bother to answer that,' she said, before he could even attempt to do so, turning to pick up her shoulder bag before standing up. 'I have to go now; I've already wasted enough of my day on this—' She broke off abruptly as Liam reached out and grasped her wrist to prevent her leaving. 'Let go of me, Liam,' she told him with cold determination.

His hand tightened about the slenderness of her wrist as he too stood up, at once dwarfing her. 'I did warn you yesterday not to believe you had got rid of me so easily.'

Her brows rose. 'And today has proved that you carry out your threats.'

His face darkened. 'It wasn't a threat—'

'Then you must have just managed to make it sound that way,' Laura scorned.

'And your decision?' His eyes were narrowed.

'Concerning your neatly engineered *fait accompli*?' she clarified derisively. 'I'm not sure,' she admitted heavily.

And she wasn't. She needed time and space—away from Liam!—to consider what she should do next. For everyone's sake, not just her own.

'Laura!' His hold on her wrist relaxed slightly, his thumb moving caressingly against the base of her own thumb now.

Laura snatched her hand out of his grasp, angry when she still felt that slight caress against her skin. 'I'll let you know, Liam,' she said tonelessly.

'When?'

'When I'm good and ready!' she returned hotly. 'You may have set this scene, Liam, but you don't have the power to dictate everyone else's moves now that you've done so! I need to think about all of this.' Definitely away from him—far away! 'When I've reached a decision I'll call you.'

He studied her flushed and angry face for several long seconds before slowly nodding his head. 'Just don't leave it too long, hmm?' he finally murmured.

Her eyes flashed in warning. 'As long as it takes! You've engineered a situation here, Liam—for your own reasons,' she added as he appeared about to protest. 'But none of us—including you!—know what the repercussions might be once this story appears in the newspaper tomorrow.' She shook her head resignedly.

Laura *didn't* know what those repercussions might be, but she could certainly take an educated guess.

She only hoped Liam was ready for it!

She hoped she was too!

CHAPTER EIGHT

PREDICTABLY, the telephone at Laura's home began ringing before eight o'clock the next morning. And continued to ring.

Laura had answered the first call, found herself talking to a reporter on a different daily newspaper from the *National Daily*, and quickly ended the conversation—only to have the phone ring again seconds later. To go unanswered. As the following dozen or so calls went unanswered, too. Until Laura decided to actually take the receiver off the hook. It meant she couldn't receive any genuine personal calls either, but in the circumstances it was a small price to pay.

How members of the press had got hold of her private home number she had no idea; she never ceased to be amazed by the amazing network that fed them.

To say she was annoyed by this intrusion was an understatement! Thank goodness Bobby was still fast asleep, no doubt exhausted by events; Laura wasn't sure how she would have answered his questions about the fact that the telephone receiver was being left permanently off the hook!

When the doorbell rang shortly after nine o'clock Laura opened the door to find one of the more determined reporters standing on her doorstep, vaguely waving his press card in her face before launching into a series of quick-fire questions. Questions Laura had no intention of answering. After telling him the inevitable 'no comment', she quietly and firmly closed the door in the young man's face.

But she could see several other reporters, some with

cameras, hovering at the end of the pathway as she did so, and her irritation turned to anger as she realised she would probably have to run the gauntlet of them if she wanted to leave the house at all today.

Her only consolation was that Liam was probably faring just as badly!

Not that she had expected her own privacy to be invaded in this way. It was Shipley Publishing the press should be talking to, not Laura Shipley herself.

Liam!

This was all his fault. If he hadn't been so determined to have his own way none of this would be happening.

The doorbell rang again.

And again, when Laura didn't move to answer it.

And yet again as she continued to stand in the hallway, glaring at the closed front door.

The incessant noise would wake Bobby in a minute, and then she was going to be really angry!

She wrenched open the door. 'I thought I told you—Liam!' she recognised, startled, as she found he was the one now standing on her doorstep, and groaned her dismay as several cameras flashed in her face. 'Come inside,' she instructed furiously, grabbing his arm to drag him into the hallway and close the door against those intruding cameras. 'What on earth are you doing here?' she demanded accusingly, knowing his presence here at her home was only going to add fuel to the fire.

Liam didn't look any happier than she did, scowling down at her darkly. 'Your telephone has been constantly engaged for the last hour,' he rasped. 'What else was I supposed to do, if I wanted to talk to you, but come over here?'

'My telephone hasn't been engaged all morning—I've taken it off the hook! A case of self-preservation,' she snapped in explanation. 'The first reporter rang here at eight o'clock this morning.' She glared her displeasure.

Liam relaxed slightly. 'They started ringing me at seven-thirty!'

Laura's eyes flashed blue-green. 'Is that supposed to make me feel better?'

He grimaced. 'If it was, it obviously hasn't succeeded.' He ran a distracted hand through the darkness of his hair. 'Are you going to ask Amy to bring us both a cup of coffee into the sitting room, or do you intend to keep me standing out here in the hallway all day?'

What she wanted to do was tell him to leave!

But he was right about the inappropriateness of them standing here in the hallway—though not for the reason he said. Even though this was a large house, their voices were no doubt carrying up the stairs to the bedrooms. And the last thing she wanted was for them to wake Bobby and for him to appear!

'Go through to the sitting room; you know the way,' she said ungraciously. 'I'll go and ask Amy for the coffee.' And check on Bobby while she was about it!

Liam was standing in front of the unlit fireplace when Laura joined him in the sitting room a few minutes later, his expression grim, although he seemed to shake that off as he turned to smile at her.

'You look much more like the old Laura in those denims,' he murmured huskily.

She felt the colour enter her cheeks. She didn't want to be reminded of the old Laura! But, as Liam had just pointed out, she was dressed casually today, in denims and a soft green jumper. Unless there was an emergency she had no intention of going in to the office today, was going to spend the time with Bobby instead.

Thoughts of her son still asleep upstairs gave a sharpness to her answer. 'Appearances can be deceptive!'

Liam raised dark brows, smiling slightly. 'Ever on the defensive, Laura.'

She gave an acknowledging inclination of her head before asking, 'Why are you here, Liam?'

His expression became grim once again, his eyes narrowed. 'Have you seen the *National Daily* today?'

She gave a disgusted snort. 'Do I need to?' She waved her hand towards the front of the house. At least half a dozen reporters and cameramen were gathered out there now.

Liam winced. 'I think so.' He pulled a folded newspaper from the pocket of his dark blue jacket, the usual denims and a tee shirt worn beneath. 'Here.' He held the newspaper out to her.

Laura sensed a certain wariness about him now, as if he already knew she was not going to like what she read in the newspaper he offered her. Her own unease deepened considerably.

'Page four,' Liam indicated as she took the newspaper.

She gasped as she turned the double-page spread to find a photograph of Liam and herself. The photograph had obviously been taken the previous afternoon at the hotel—without either of them realising it! The two of them were seated in the hotel lounge, smiling across at each other in what looked like a very friendly manner.

Laura couldn't imagine at what part of their meeting *that* had been, but nevertheless the evidence was there in front of her eyes.

She looked up accusingly at Liam. 'Your little friend was very busy yesterday afternoon! Did you know about this photograph being taken?' she accused.

'Certainly not,' he replied in a voice that brooked no arguments on that score. 'But, damning as the photograph is, I think you should read the article that goes with it before making further comment,' he suggested.

Laura shot him another narrow-eyed glance before turning her attention to the newspaper article, the colour slowly leaving her cheeks as she read.

> Mrs. Laura Shipley, head of Shipley Publishing, preferred to make no comment on the suggestion that she would shortly be publishing a new, long-awaited novel by Liam O'Reilly. But the couple, photographed together yesterday afternoon, certainly seem to have a close relationship. Perhaps it could soon be wedding bells for the widow of the late Robert Shipley, mother of the Shipley heir, Robert Shipley Junior, and the world-famous Irish author, Liam O'Reilly…?

Laura felt sick, her hands shaking so badly she had to put the newspaper down on the coffee table. Where had Janey Wilson got all that information? More to the point, look what she had done with it. This was worse, so much worse, than she could ever have imagined.

She swallowed down her nausea, half afraid to raise her head and look at Liam. So much for her not wanting Liam to even know she had a son!

'I'm sorry, Laura.' Liam was the one to finally speak.

'*You're* sorry?' she flashed, looking up to glare at him. 'How do you think I feel?'

Liam winced at the unmistakable anger in her voice. 'I had no idea Janey intended printing something like that.' He looked disgustedly towards the open newspaper.

'She may be the sister of an old university friend, Liam,'

Laura told him sternly, 'but she is obviously first and foremost a reporter!'

Anger was a much easier option than the tears she really felt like shedding. Tears of sheer frustration. How dared that woman print those private details about her life?

'Obviously.' Liam sighed. 'I—' He broke off as Amy arrived with the tray of coffee. 'Laura might need a brandy to go with that?' He looked at her enquiringly.

'At nine-thirty in the morning? No, thank you,' Laura refused. 'Thank you, Amy.' Her voice softened as she spoke to her housekeeper before Amy returned to the kitchen.

'Shall I pour?' Liam offered as Laura made no effort to do so.

'Go ahead,' Laura invited uncaringly, pacing the room as her thoughts raced.

There was no way Liam could have overlooked that mention of Bobby in the last sentence of the newspaper article. Not that it really told him anything except that she had a son, but she would have preferred that he didn't even know that much!

And as for that reference to wedding bells for Liam and herself—!

No wonder celebrities got so angry at some of the things the press wrote about them. She and Liam had only been drinking coffee together, and yet Janey Wilson's article implied so much more.

'Here.' Liam put a cup of coffee into her hand now. 'I know you don't take sugar, but I've put some in anyway. I think you need the energy boost.'

So he remembered how she took her coffee too. Strange, it afforded Laura no satisfaction that he had shown his own remembrance of their past relationship.

The sweetened coffee tasted awful, but Liam had been

right about the energy boost making her feel slightly better. She now felt she had enough strength to administer the slap on the face he deserved!

'Uh-oh.' Liam eyed her warily over the rim of his own coffee cup as he pretended to back away. 'Perhaps I put a little too much sugar in your coffee; I certainly recognise that light of battle in your beautiful eyes!'

Laura couldn't help it—she laughed. He really was the most irritating, arrogant, attractive man she had ever met in her life. His blue eyes had darkened teasingly; the hard strength of his face had softened in amusement. Even if she had no intention of being affected by that attraction!

'This isn't funny, Liam,' she rebuked. Although even to her own ears she sounded less than convincing.

'No, it isn't,' he agreed heavily. 'I've already spoken to Janey, told her exactly what I think of her half-truths and innuendos—'

'For all the good it will have done you.' Laura sighed. 'She'll probably print another story tomorrow along the lines of you doth protest to much!'

Liam scowled. 'I think I've made it more than clear to Janey that if she prints another word about the two of us I'll personally wring her neck for her!'

Laura grimaced. 'I don't think silencing Janey Wilson will have achieved much.' She glanced pointedly towards the front of the house, where the reporters were still gathered. 'I believe they already have several photographs of you arriving at my home to spice up another article for tomorrow's newspapers!'

'I really had no idea this would develop into such a circus.' He shook his head disgustedly.

'The press are even more vociferous now than they were eight years ago,' she opined.

'Obviously, if even a friend like Janey can make something out of nothing,' Liam replied.

Laura gave the ghost of a smile, nodding ruefully. 'Perhaps you should have told her she's eight years out of date where we're concerned.'

As soon as she had made the remark she wished she could take the words back. The atmosphere had suddenly changed between them, charged with an awareness now that hadn't been there before. An awareness of each other, of what they had once been to each other…

Liam put down his empty cup, taking a step towards her. 'Is she?' he said as he stood only inches away from Laura. 'I'm not so sure about that,' he said softly, one of his hands reaching up to cup the side of her face. 'You're more beautiful than ever, Laura,' he groaned.

She was barely breathing, her gaze locked with Liam's. The ticking of the clock that stood above the fireplace suddenly seemed very loud and intrusive. Her heart, she knew, was beating a much quicker pattern.

She shook her head. 'I don't think this is a good idea, Liam,' she murmured throatily.

'You're not a child any longer, Laura—'

'I never was a child where you were concerned,' she protested.

'Oh, yes, you were.' His gaze moved slowly over the perfection of her face, the darkness of her hair, before returning to the softness of her mouth. 'But you're a woman now, Laura. A mother, too,' he added gruffly, looking down at her with gentle enquiry. 'I knew there was something different about you when we met again, something that couldn't just be attributed to eight years' maturity. Obviously being a mother suits you.'

It didn't suit her; it was what she was. It was all she really wanted to be, and Bobby was the centre of her life.

'Why didn't you tell me about your son, Laura?' Liam prompted softly.

'I didn't want to bore you; you've made your views on children more than plain,' she scorned to hide her rising panic. She did not want to discuss Bobby!

'Only having any of my own,' Liam refuted. 'How old is Robert, Laura? Does he look like you?'

Her mouth had gone very dry, and the beating of her heart sounded louder than ever. She didn't want to answer any of these questions. Wouldn't answer them!

'We call him Bobby. Robert was too confusing when it was his father's name too,' she responded.

Only to witness the tightening of Liam's mouth, that nerve pulsing in his throat once again. Obviously he didn't like this reference to Bobby's father, Laura's late husband.

But even though Robert hadn't been Bobby's biological father he had been in every other sense there was. Robert had been beside her during her pregnancy, with her during Bobby's birth, and had involved himself totally in Bobby's babyhood and infancy, often reaching the baby's cotside quicker than Laura if Bobby had wakened in the night. Robert *had* been Bobby's father!

Laura moved determinedly away from Liam, turning as his hand fell back to his side. 'I believe we have much more important things to discuss than my son.' She felt an inward jolt at the possessiveness in her tone. But Bobby *was* her son, and with Robert gone she felt he was hers alone!

'I would like to meet him,' Liam suggested.

She turned to him sharply. 'Why?'

'Why not?'

Calm down, Laura, she told herself steadily, breathing deeply. 'It's been a difficult time for Bobby since his father died,' she reasoned. 'Losing a parent at such a young age has made him all the more attached to the one he has left; I don't like to confuse him with transient friends.' Even to her own ears that sounded like a deliberate slap in the face, and she could see by the tightening of Liam's mouth and the narrowing of his eyes that he had recognised it as such.

His head went back challengingly. 'Is that why you keep the man currently sharing your bed as a separate part of your life?'

A retaliatory slap! Probably deserved after her own remark, Laura accepted. But it wasn't one she was going to give him the satisfaction of reacting to!

Her lips pursed. 'Surely, Liam, that's a contradiction in terms?' she countered. 'If this mythical man were sharing my bed, then I wouldn't be able to keep him as a separate part of my life?'

His eyes had narrowed questioningly. 'Mythical?' he prompted softly.

She had fallen into his trap yet again! Trust Liam to pounce on the one word that was of any real interest to him!

She changed tack. 'You're the one who keeps insisting there has to be a man somewhere.'

'Only because I don't believe it's a woman,' Liam responded. 'And you are far too beautiful to have been completely on your own the last two years. Unless those were the ''transient friends'' you were referring to earlier?' he added derisively.

Oh, this man was so insulting! And under any other circumstances she would have told him exactly what he could do with his rude remarks. But here, in her home, with Bobby only feet away and likely to appear downstairs without warning, her one real wish was to have Liam leave as soon as possible.

'I'm not even going to qualify that remark with an answer, Liam,' she returned. 'Now, if you've quite finished...? I have things to do today.' Although none of them involved leaving the house; she had no intention of running the gauntlet where those hovering reporters were concerned!

Liam's eyes were glacial. 'Like explaining to the current man that this newspaper report is an exaggeration?' he challenged.

Laura eyed him coolly. 'I very rarely explain myself to anyone these days, Liam.' And especially not him! 'And that newspaper article isn't an exaggeration; it's an outright fabrication!' she stated firmly.

'It needn't be,' Liam told her gruffly, suddenly close to her once again.

Too close!

He shouldn't be here in her home at all, let alone standing only inches away from her. She was actually able to feel the heat given off by his body.

A body she had once known more intimately than she knew her own...!

Where had that come from? She groaned inwardly. She didn't want to remember the intimacies she had shared with Liam eight years ago!

Sometimes in the night, with sleep sweeping away her defences, those memories came back in her dreams, and the ecstasy she had once known in his arms was undeniable then. And when she woke in the morning, much as she hated herself for it, her body would still burn and ache from that remembered pleasure.

'Laura...!' Liam whispered now, his arms moving about the slenderness of her waist as he drew her close to him, his eyes searching on the flushed beauty of her face before his head lowered and his mouth took possession of hers.

Senses already heightened by those thoughts of the past,

Laura was instantly swept away on a tide of pleasure, her body arching into the hardness of his, her lips opening as Liam deepened the kiss, his tongue moving searchingly.

They fitted together like two halves of a whole!

Laura's height was no match for Liam's six feet four inches, but the softness of her curves fitted into the muscular hollows of his body, her breasts against his chest, thighs pressed into the hardness of his.

And her body remembered, as she remembered, the pleasure of that hardness. She felt a warm rush between her thighs even as Liam continued to sip and taste her lips.

His hands moved restlessly across the slenderness of her back, fingers seeking the warm flesh beneath the green jumper, moving round to cup the softness of her breast against the silky material of her bra, the nipple instantly hard, throbbing hotly as a thumbtip gently caressed her.

Liam moaned low in his throat as his own body hardened in response, hands shaking slightly now as they tightened about the narrowness of her waist, pulling her even closer against him.

His lips left hers to trail over the creaminess of her cheek, before travelling down the column of her throat to the sensitive hollows below.

Laura was now feeling dizzy with desire. Her hands clung to the width of his shoulders to stop herself from falling. She was aware only of Liam and the moist caress of his lips, his teeth gently nibbling an earlobe, sending arrows of warm ecstasy to every part of her body.

'Mummy? Mummy, where are you?'

The sound of Bobby's voice calling out to Laura from the hallway had the same effect on her as having a bucket of ice-cold water thrown over her would have done!

She sprang guiltily away from Liam, the pleasure she had known in his arms only seconds earlier completely obliterated as she heard the soft pad of Bobby's slipper-clad feet as he approached the sitting room.

Any second now, Liam and Bobby were going to come face to face with each other. And in her slightly befuddled state Laura couldn't think of a single thing she could do or say to prevent it happening!

CHAPTER NINE

'MUMMY!' A relieved Bobby appeared in the doorway, obviously pleased to have found her at last, although his dark blue eyes instantly moved curiously to the man in the room with her.

'Hello, darling.' Laura smiled, moving to his side, totally ignoring Liam—and what had just occurred between the two of them!—as she bent down to give her son a hug. 'Feeling better now?' she prompted gently, looking at Bobby searchingly.

Apart from a little bump on his head, and a slightly sore knee, he didn't seem to have suffered too much harm from his accident. His long night's sleep had obviously refreshed him too; this morning there was colour back in the previous paleness of his cheeks, and his eyes were bright and alert.

Eyes that were fixed now on the man who stood in front of the window. Bobby's expression was slightly shy as he looked at this stranger.

Laura drew in a deep breath before turning, her arm protectively about Bobby's narrow shoulders as she held him to her side, her expression slightly challenging as she looked across at Liam. A Liam whose expression was totally unreadable as he looked not at her, but down at Bobby.

Laura tried to see the little boy through Liam's eyes. Still dressed in his pyjamas, Bobby was tall for his age, with a thinness that resulted from an abundance of energy and not lack of food. His hair was dark and slightly curly, dark blue eyes fringed by lashes of the same dark colour.

Colouring that could just as well be her own, Laura decided stubbornly.

But could she also claim the facial features that already promised to look so much like Liam's as Bobby matured? Or the mischievous grin that could be so like Liam's?

If challenged, she would have to!

'Your mother seems to be temporarily speechless, Bobby.' Liam was the first one to speak, only the huskiness of his voice giving any indication of the passion they had so recently shared. 'So I had better introduce myself. I'm Liam O'Reilly.' He moved forward to hold his hand out formally to the little boy. 'An old friend of your mother's.'

'Robert William Shipley Junior,' Bobby told him with shy pride as he shook the proffered hand.

Laura felt an emotional catch in her throat as father and son faced each other for the first time. They were so alike. Liam *must* realise who Bobby was!

Or maybe it was just her, with her inner knowledge, who could see the likeness? She certainly hoped so…!

Liam released Bobby's hand as he smiled down at him 'Your mother tells me you prefer to be called Bobby,' he said softly.

The little boy shrugged narrow shoulders. 'I don't mind Bobby or Robert. The teachers at school call me Robert.'

Laura looked down at her son in some surprise. Bobby had never told her that before. But perhaps now that his father, also Robert, was dead…

'I think I quite like Bobby, if that's okay with you?' Liam spoke to the little boy, but his narrowed gaze was fixed on Laura. As if he was well aware of how perplexed she had just felt.

And maybe he was, she inwardly conceded; Liam, as an author, was a people-watcher, had always been able to intuitively read other people's emotions.

Which was yet another reason for guarding her own emotions when around him!

She straightened her shoulders. 'If that's all, Liam,' she prompted distantly, wanting him to leave. 'I would like to go and share some breakfast with Bobby now.'

'Breakfast sounds like a good idea,' Liam came back smoothly. 'I didn't feel much like eating earlier this morning,' he elaborated, as Laura gave him a frowning look.

Because he had been bombarded with reporters at his hotel even earlier than she had!

But, even so, her suggestion about breakfast had not included Liam. And he knew it!

'We're only eating cereal and toast,' she told him flatly.

'Sounds good,' Liam replied. 'As long as you have those cornflakes with the sugar already on them; they're my favourite,' he told Bobby conspiratorially.

'Mine, too,' Bobby told him with a gappy grin. He was missing his two top front teeth, being at the age when he was starting to lose his milk teeth in favour of permanent ones.

Laura looked down in puzzlement at her son; this was the first she had heard of that particular cereal being Bobby's favourite. But, with no permanent male figure in his life, she accepted that Bobby was likely to suffer a few cases of hero-worship over the following years. It was just that Liam was the last person she wanted Bobby to see in that role!

'It looks like it's sugar-coated cornflakes all round, Laura,' Liam told her with satisfaction, already following Bobby towards the kitchen.

Laura followed much more slowly. Did Liam know who Bobby really was? If he did, he was giving no indication of it. Which was even more disquieting.

Amy raised surprised brows in her direction when Laura

entered the kitchen. Liam was already seated at the pine table in there as Bobby got out the cereal, bowls and milk, putting them on the table before sitting down himself.

Laura gave the housekeeper a resigned shrug. There was really nothing else she could do; she couldn't exactly throw Liam bodily out of the house. Besides, she was still uneasy about how much Liam might or might not have guessed about Bobby's parentage…

'Shouldn't a big boy like you be at school today?' Liam asked Bobby once the two of them had their bowls of cereal.

'I fell over two days ago and bumped my head,' Bobby said. 'I had to stay in hospital overnight. But Mummy stayed with me.' He looked up at Laura for confirmation of this momentous event in his young life.

'I certainly did.' She ruffled the darkness of his hair with gentle affection, looking up challengingly at Liam as she sensed his gaze on her.

So that's where you rushed off to two days ago, his eyes clearly said.

Laura gave him a withering glance before turning away. She had told him the man in her life he kept referring to was mythical; it was Liam's own fault if he hadn't believed her.

'Sit down and eat some breakfast.'

Angry colour flooded her cheeks at Liam's dictatorial tone. She would eat breakfast when she was good and ready, not when he told her to. Who did he think—?

'Please?' he added cajolingly, blue gaze on her flushed cheeks.

Laura sat. Until she had spoken to him alone, found out whether or not he had guessed that Bobby was his son, then she didn't particularly want to antagonise him. Although his manner seemed rather too pleasant for that of a man who had just realised he had a son he knew nothing about…

It was impossible to tell with Liam. Able to read and gauge other people's emotions, he also had the ability to completely hide his own behind an inscrutable mask. That mask was firmly in place at the moment!

Liam continued to talk to Bobby as Laura drank her coffee and ate a slice of toast, encouraging the little boy to talk about school, and his friends there.

Laura's own troubled thoughts drifted as her wariness increased.

'—think you would really like Ireland, Bobby.' Liam's suggestion brought Laura's wandering attention back to their conversation.

What did he mean, Bobby would like Ireland? She had no plans ever to take her son there!

Liam turned to look at her with expressionless eyes as he sensed her renewed attention. 'Bobby was just telling me that he likes it when you and he go out for a drive at weekends so that the two of you can go for walks in the countryside,' he explained. 'There's nowhere quite like Ireland for beautiful countryside and peaceful walks,' he opined.

That might or might not be true—Laura had no intention of visiting Ireland to find out! 'I think after Bobby's accident our walks will have to wait for a while,' she replied—firmly stamping on any suggestion that Liam might join them this weekend before he even made it!

'Your mother is probably right,' Liam told Bobby as the little boy looked about to protest. 'Mothers usually are,' he added enigmatically.

Laura gave him a sharp look, surprised that he had actually agreed with her concerning the walks, but equally puzzled by his last remark, although she could see no mockery or sarcasm in his expression.

She stood up abruptly. 'If you've finished breakfast, I think it's time I took Bobby upstairs for a bath...'

'Oh, but, Mummy—'

'Remember what I said about mothers.' Liam teasingly interrupted Bobby's protest, standing up as he did so. 'It's time I was going anyway. But I'll come and see you again, Bobby, if that's okay with you?'

Laura gave him another look. She didn't want Liam and Bobby becoming any closer than they were...!

'Great!' Again Bobby gave Liam that toothless grin.

'Upstairs, young man,' Laura told her son firmly. 'While I see Liam to the door.'

Bobby followed them out into the hallway, running up the stairs with all the exuberance of his youth.

'There doesn't look too much wrong with him now,' Liam remarked as he watched Bobby disappear up to his bedroom. 'What happened?' he prompted, turning back to her.

'A fall at school. Nothing's broken, though, so he should be back at school on Monday.'

'He's a fine-looking boy, Laura.'

She swallowed hard, reluctant to look up into the hard handsomeness of Liam's face. A face that, after seeing the two of them together like this, was so obviously—to her, at least!—a mature version of Bobby's...

She drew in a deep breath, lifting her head in defiance. 'I like to think so.'

'You must be very proud of him.' Liam gave an acknowledging inclination of his head.

'Very,' she confirmed curtly, still uncertain of where this conversation was leading. If Liam had seen Bobby's likeness to him, guessed that he was actually his son, why didn't he just say so?

'Have dinner with me, Laura,' Liam said instead.

Her eyes widened in alarm. 'I can't leave Bobby—'

'Not tonight,' Liam interrupted. 'I realise that at the moment Bobby is your first priority, that for today, at least, he needs all your attention. But tomorrow is Saturday; I'm sure by then he'll be settled enough for you to leave him with Amy for a few hours. By that time you will probably welcome the break too,' he added as she would have protested once again.

Laua's mouth closed with a snap. Since when had Liam become so attuned to another person's feelings? He was certainly showing more sensitivity than she had ever known from him before.

But did she want to have dinner with him, tomorrow or any other evening?

The answer to that was a definite no! But there was much more at stake than her own feelings…

'In that case…thank you. Dinner sounds fine,' she accepted tersely. 'But could you find somewhere discreet for us to eat? I don't relish the idea of having reporters leering all over us!'

Liam's face tightened at this reminder of the reporters waiting outside the house. 'Don't worry, I'll make sure it's somewhere no one will recognise us.'

Very few people would recognise her anyway—at least, until that photograph of the two of them had appeared in the newspaper today they wouldn't have done!—but Liam was another proposition altogether. But he had issued the invitation; it was up to him to find the venue.

Not that it was a dinner Laura was particularly looking forward to. She just felt in the circumstances, until she had ascertained exactly how much Liam had guessed about

Bobby's true parentage, that it might be better to meet Liam halfway. Dinner together sounded harmless enough.

Although, as she had discovered only too well this morning, what sounded harmless didn't always turn out that way. Who would have thought, when Liam had arrived so unexpectedly this morning, that the two of them would end up in each other's arms before he left again…!

'It will be a business dinner, Liam,' she told him firmly.

His brows rose mockingly. 'Will it?'

'There's no other reason for the two of us to meet.'

'If you say so.'

Laura frowned darkly. 'Liam—'

'Your son is waiting upstairs for you to bath him,' he cut in dryly, reaching out to lightly grasp her shoulders. 'If mothers are usually right, then little boys shouldn't be kept waiting!'

She was very aware of the warmth of his hands on her shoulders. 'How about big boys?' she teased.

Liam shrugged, his mouth thinning grimly. 'We're just as impatient for what we want, but we've learnt to hide it better!'

'And what do you want, Liam?' she prompted softly.

He grimaced. 'Like most people, what I apparently can't have.' He sighed heavily. 'Tell me, Laura, do you hate me very much?'

She drew in a shocked breath at his words. Hate him? Of course she didn't— Well…maybe eight years ago for a while she had, she accepted. But that was so long ago, and her successful marriage to Robert, Bobby's birth, had more than compensated for that.

'I have too much in my life that's good to feel hate towards anyone,' she answered truthfully.

Liam looked down at her with assessing eyes. 'Did you love Robert Shipley?' he ground out harshly.

Her face softened with the remembrance of that love, eyes glittering with unshed tears. 'Very much,' she responded.

'He must have been quite something.' Liam nodded, his hands dropping away from her shoulders. 'I would like to know more about him.'

Laura looked up at him warily. 'Why?'

'Because you loved him!' Liam rasped harshly.

'I see no connection between the two things.' She shook her head uncomprehendingly. 'I certainly see no point in the two of us talking about my husband.'

'No?' Liam glanced up the stairs. 'From the little Bobby said about him over breakfast, he obviously adored him too.'

'Why shouldn't he have done? He was his father!'

Too defensive, Laura, she instantly rebuked herself with a pained wince. But she couldn't help it. There was much more to being a father than the mere act of bringing a child into being. And Robert had more than filled all those other roles necessary for being a father.

'Yes, he was,' Liam conceded gruffly. 'I'll call for you here tomorrow night about eight o'clock, shall I?'

The sudden change of subject threw Laura for a few seconds. Would she ever be able to keep up with this man's change of moods…?

'I don't think that's a good idea.' She shook her head. 'If, as I suspect, there's going to be more speculation about the two of us in tomorrow's newspapers, then it would be better if we weren't seen leaving my home together tomorrow evening.'

'Good point,' Liam conceded. 'Okay, I'll telephone here tomorrow with the name of the restaurant. If you don't mind meeting me there…?'

'Why should I mind?' she replied. 'As I've said, as far as I'm concerned it's business.'

His mouth twisted into a humourless smile. 'There's no need to belabour the point, Laura; I heard you the first time.'

He might have heard her, but she just wanted to make sure he understood!

'I won't come to the door, if you don't mind,' she said. 'I think the press have enough photographs of the two of us together for one day!' And she hated to think what they were going to do with them!

Although that was the least of her troubles as she walked up the stairs a few minutes later. Dinner with Liam tomorrow evening definitely headed that particular list!

'When I said somewhere discreet, Liam,' she snapped, 'I did not mean your hotel suite!'

She looked around them pointedly, at the dining table in the sitting room of his suite elegantly set for two people to dine, the crystal glasses, the cutlery gleaming silver, a vase of red roses in the centre of the highly polished table.

Liam had telephoned the house earlier and spoken to Amy, as Laura and Bobby had gone out to buy Bobby a toy, asking Laura to meet him at his hotel at eight o'clock. Laura had assumed—mistakenly it now turned out!—that the two of them would be going on to a restaurant from there. One glance at that elegant set dinner table had shown her how wrong she was!

'Don't look so accusing, Laura,' Liam responded impatiently. He was wearing a black dinner jacket, snowy white shirt and black bow tie, his hair still damp from the shower he had recently taken. 'I don't have an ulterior motive for deciding it was easier to eat here; I tried all the restaurants

I thought fitted your description and they were all fully booked.'

She gave him a scathing glance, very aware that her glittering figure-hugging gold dress, with its short length that showed the long expanse of her slender legs—chosen as a boost to her own confidence rather than any sort of come-on!—seemed slightly out of place in the intimacy of this hotel suite. *Liam's* hotel suite!

'Didn't you explain that you're Liam O'Reilly?' she threw back totally put out by the fact that she was expected to eat here alone with Liam in the intimacy of his hotel suite.

His expression darkened at her deliberate antagonism. 'I've never worked that way,' he rasped coldly. 'Look,' he sighed, 'I know you aren't happy with this arrangement—'

'You have no idea how unhappy it makes me,' she muttered grimly.

'But the alternative was to cancel the whole thing—and to me that was no alternative at all!'

Her eyes sparkled angrily as she glared across at him. 'Maybe you should have given me the benefit of choosing for myself!'

His mouth twisted furiously. 'And we both know what choice you would have made!'

She was breathing hard in her agitation, not at all pleased at the thought of spending the evening here alone with Liam.

She was still uncertain as to the reason for this dinner invitation, had been uneasy about it all day, and feeling herself cornered like this, without even the distraction of other diners to alleviate some of the awkwardness, had not improved those feelings of unease.

'This is impossible, Liam.' She shook her head.

'Why is it?' he reasoned impatiently.

'Don't be deliberately obtuse,' she returned. 'Did you see the newspapers this morning?'

Liam sighed, picking up the opened bottle of chilled white wine to pour some of the fruity liquid into two glasses. 'Of course I saw them,' he said evenly, handing her one of the glasses before taking a sip from his own. 'They would have been hard to miss.'

As Laura had guessed, photographs of Liam arriving at her home yesterday morning had appeared on the front page of several of the more sensational tabloids, and speculation about their relationship, both professional and personal, was continuing.

'Then you must see,' she said impatiently, 'that the two of us having dinner together in your hotel suite will only add to the rumour that we're—that we're—'

'We're what, Laura?' Liam interrupted, dropping down into one of the armchairs to look up at her with mocking blue eyes.

'Involved!' she spat the word out angrily.

He raised dark brows. 'And…?'

'We aren't!' Laura bit out through gritted teeth. Liam wasn't just being obtuse now, he was being deliberately awkward!

He shrugged broad shoulders. 'Not through lack of trying on my part.'

She gasped, colour heating her cheeks. 'You—I—'

'Yes, you and I,' Liam repeated softly, standing up to put his glass down on the coffee table before slowly walking towards her. 'Is that such an awful idea?' He came to a halt only inches away from her, his eyes navy blue now as he looked down at her.

'Awful?' she repeated incredulously. 'It's ludicrous!' she told him heatedly.

Liam's mouth tightened, his eyes narrowing. 'Why?' he prompted huskily.

'Not again, Liam!' She moved sharply away as he would have reached out and grasped her shoulders, moving to the other side of the room. 'Yesterday morning was a—a mistake. With maturity I've come to try not to repeat my mistakes,' she added challengingly.

'Believe it or not, I'm trying, in my own way, to do the same thing.'

Laura gave him a sharp look. Exactly what did he mean by that remark?

'Through my own stupidity I let you slip through my fingers eight years ago, Laura,' he said quietly, answering her unasked question. 'I don't intend letting it happen a second time.'

Laura could feel her cheeks paling as she stared across at him with wide disbelieving eyes. She might have told him this was a business dinner, but she had really come here purely to discover what he might or might not have realised about Bobby's parentage, and for no other reason. Hadn't she…?

As she looked at Liam, so handsome in his evening attire, the warmth in his eyes for her alone, she began to question her own self-honesty. Had part of her, the part of her that also remembered how good they had been together eight years ago, ached to know whether it would still be the same between them? If their response to each other yesterday morning was anything to go by, then she could have no doubts about that!

But had she been aware of that when she'd dressed to come out this evening? Had her motives in wearing this gold dress, a dress that she knew suited her dark colouring and the slenderness of her figure, been as self-orientated as she had told herself they were at the time?

As she looked up into Liam's face, her own gaze locked with mesmerising blue eyes, she didn't know any more!

She moistened dry lips. 'Liam—'

'Laura, won't you give me a chance to make up for the past?' he cut in. 'I was an idiot; I freely admit that. But don't even idiots deserve a second chance?'

A second chance to do what? Ruin her life once again? To just disappear when it suited him, never to be heard from again?

She shuddered just at the thought of going through that again. Not again.

Never again!

'Laura!' Liam reached her side in two long strides, having watched the emotions flickering across her face, reaching out to grasp her shoulders, shaking her slightly as she refused to look up at him. 'Won't you at least give me a chance to try to make amends for—?'

'No!' she finally gasped, shaking her head in firm denial as she glared up at him. 'I like my life just the way it is, Liam. I do not want you around, with your egotistical arrogance, cluttering it up!' She was deliberately nasty, wanting to put an emotional barrier between them even if, with Liam's close proximity, she couldn't get a physical one.

He became very still, looking down at her searchingly. 'You lied to me yesterday morning, Laura,' he finally said heavily, his hands slowly dropping away from her shoulders.

She shivered involuntarily at the removal of that warmth. 'In what way did I lie?' she challenged hardly, afraid of what his answer might be. If he were referring to Bobby—!

He drew in a harsh breath, grim lines beside his nose and mouth. 'You do hate me,' he said tonelessly. 'But I can assure you it's no more than I hate myself for the idiot I was eight years ago.'

He wasn't talking about Bobby! Her relief at this realisation superceded everything else.

'I didn't lie, Liam,' she told him, almost gently. 'I really don't hate you. But neither do I wish to be involved with you again,' she added with finality.

Even if she might have some residual feelings left for Liam—and after the way she had responded to him yesterday morning she must have!—she must never lose sight of the fact that any involvement with him was a possible danger to her own relationship with Bobby.

'Fair enough.' Liam held his hands up in supplication.

Laura eyed him uncertainly. Had he accepted her decision just a little too readily to be sincere…?

Or was it her hurt pride that was reacting now? Surely she didn't really want him to keep up this personal pursuit?

As she had already told Liam, there was no point. It might just be that part of her that was still smarting from his desertion eight years ago that felt a certain sense of satisfaction in the knowledge that their roles had now been reversed; Liam obviously wanted a relationship with her now, and she was the one repulsing him.

Not very nice sentiments, she inwardly rebuked. Not nice at all.

She put up a hand to her temple, which had begun to pound painfully. 'I think, in the circumstances, I'll give dinner a miss, if you don't mind…?'

He nodded abruptly, eyes reflecting nothing but the room about them, his expression also unreadable. 'I think that might be a good idea.'

Laura bent to pick up her evening bag from the table she had placed it on when she arrived. Such a short time ago.

But a lot had happened in that half an hour or so. Primarily, Liam was once again going out of her life.

She should be glad. Should feel nothing but relief at having the pressure of his presence removed from her life once and for all.

She paused beside the door. 'What do you intend doing about the book, Liam?' She looked at him with inquisitive eyes.

He shrugged. 'You've assured me Perry is an excellent editor; I have no reason to doubt you.'

Her eyes widened. 'You're agreeable to his being your editor now? To Shipley publishing your book?' She couldn't quite believe this easy acquiescence. It wasn't like the Liam she knew at all!

His mouth twisted into a humourless smile. 'I'm not as completely unreasonable as you seem to think I am.'

No, but he had gone to so much trouble to try and achieve his own way, had even involved the newspapers—something he had told her he didn't want under any circumstances. There was definitely something not quite right about this!

'Liam—'

'Laura?' he came back smoothly.

Her feelings of unease increased. He was too smooth, too calm, too everything! 'You'll come in to see Perry on Monday?'

'I will,' he agreed, sounding very Irish. 'After which I have to return to Ireland.'

Not only was he agreeing to accept Perry as his editor, but he was removing himself from London—and her life—as well. There had to be a catch in this somewhere!

'I wish you had looked this pleased to see me again!' Liam chuckled self-derisively at her obvious relief at his going. 'I will be back, Laura. There are still things to do concerning the book.'

Yes, but she didn't have to be involved in them now…

Why didn't she leave? She had said she was going to, and yet she had made no effort yet to open the door and go.

Possibly because she felt that once she left here tonight she would never see this particular Liam again. The professional writer Liam O'Reilly, yes, but not this man who had pursued her so relentlessly the last few days.

Oh, she didn't know what she wanted any more! She had been telling Liam for those same few days that she wasn't interested in renewing their past relationship, yet now that he had accepted her decision she hesitated about leaving him.

She set her shoulders determinedly. 'Goodbye, Liam,' she told him firmly.

'Goodbye, Laura.' His expression was still unreadable.

Her feet felt as if they were weighted down by lead, her movements slow and sluggish. But finally she managed to open the door and walk out into the hotel corridor, closing the door firmly behind her.

And closing the door to that compartment of her heart that contained her repressed feelings for Liam—the door he had been trying so hard to prise open…!

CHAPTER TEN

'I CAN'T believe I slept until this time!' Laura exclaimed self-disgustedly as she entered the kitchen at ten o'clock the next morning to find Amy already preparing the vegetables for lunch.

Amy turned to give her a warm smile. 'You obviously needed the rest,' she volunteered.

No, it hadn't been that at all. When Laura had arrived home shortly after nine o'clock last night she had gone straight to her bedroom. But not to sleep. Not that she hadn't tried to sleep, to push everything but Bobby and her work from her mind. But memories of Liam, both from the past and the present, had kept intruding, making it impossible for her to relax enough to go to sleep. Consequently it had been the early hours of the morning before she'd fallen into a fitful slumber, resulting in her completely oversleeping this morning.

'Where's Bobby?' She had checked his bedroom before coming downstairs, and the morning room on her way past, expecting him to be in there watching television. The only other place she could think of him being was the kitchen, with Amy, but he wasn't in here either…

'Mr O'Reilly called in at nine o'clock—'

'Liam did?' Laura questioned sharply, a terrible sinking feeling developing in the pit of her stomach.

'He brought a kite with him,' Amy went on, frowning at Laura's obvious shock. 'He thought Bobby might like to go with him—'

'You've let Liam take Bobby out?' Laura gasped, paling.

'Into the garden to fly it,' Amy finished. 'I would never let anyone take Bobby out without your permission,' she added with gentle rebuke.

Laura sank down into one of the kitchen chairs, some of the colour returning to her cheeks. 'Of course you wouldn't,' she realised self-disgustedly, her colour receding again as the full import of Amy's words sank in. 'Liam is out in the garden—this garden!—flying a kite with Bobby?'

The housekeeper nodded. 'As Mr O'Reilly said, it's a nice windy day for it.'

It certainly was—but what was Liam doing here at all? Hadn't they decided last night that the less they saw of each other the better?

Not exactly, she realised slowly. She had told Liam she didn't want to become personally involved with him again. A statement, she remembered thinking at the time, that he had seemed to accept too readily… A statement he had taken to its literal limit; she hadn't included Bobby's name!

She stood up hurriedly. 'I think I'll just go and check on the two of them.'

'They were having a great time when I looked out at them a couple of minutes ago,' Amy assured her. 'Have a cup of coffee before you go out; you always say you need a couple of cups to be able to start the day properly.'

What Laura had actually said was that she needed a couple of cups of coffee in the morning to help her feel human!

She raised dark brows at Amy, her mouth quirking self-derisively. 'You think I'm overreacting?'

The housekeeper hesitated. 'That depends on what you're reacting to…'

Laura swallowed hard, sitting down abruptly as Amy placed the cup of strong coffee on the table in front of her. 'How long have you known?'

The housekeeper smiled. 'I'm not sure that I do know.

Not really. Of course I've always known that Mr Robert wasn't Bobby's father. We both know that was never even a possibility. But as to who Bobby's biological father really is…' She shrugged. 'In every other sense of the word Mr Robert *was* his father.'

'But…?' Laura prompted warily.

'I was struck by the resemblance between Bobby and Mr O'Reilly from the moment I first opened the door to Mr O'Reilly earlier in the week.' Amy admitted gently. 'That's the reason I was unsure about whether or not to let him wait to see you.'

Laura had thought that unusual at the time…

'What must you think of me, Amy?' She buried her face in her hands.

The older woman's arm came about her shoulders. 'I think you, and Bobby, helped to make the last five years of Mr Robert's life the happiest he had ever known,' she told her emotionally.

Laura looked up through a haze of tears. 'Did we? Did we really?' She so much hoped so, after all that Robert had done for her.

'Don't ever doubt it,' Amy said with certainty. 'A family, a child of his own to love and care for, were things Mr Robert had long ago accepted he would never have. I know that he looked on both of you as a gift,' she said. 'A gift he wasn't sure he deserved, but one that he cherished above everything else.'

Laura swallowed hard. 'If anyone deserved a loving family, Robert did.'

'And you gave him that, Laura; never doubt it for a moment,' the housekeeper told her firmly. 'As to Mr O'Reilly, I'm sure you had your own reasons for not marrying him eight years ago.'

Laura gave a humourless smile. 'A very good reason, Amy. He never asked me!'

The older woman raised blonde brows. 'Some men aren't very good at responsibility—'

'He never knew about Bobby, Amy.' Laura felt compelled to defend him.

The other woman looked concerned. 'That would no longer seem to be the case,' she observed ruefully, looking in the direction of the garden, where Liam was now flying a kite with his son.

Laura looked up at her. 'You think Liam knows?' her voice was hushed.

'Don't you?'

'I have no idea,' she burst out. 'If he does know, he hasn't said anything. And it isn't the sort of thing I can come straight out and ask him!' Especially as she would prefer it if Liam *didn't* know! 'If Liam does know, Amy, then why hasn't he said anything?' she asked emotionally.

The housekeeper paused, straightened, and then replied, 'I think you would have to ask him that.'

But she couldn't, not without revealing the truth herself. And it was a truth she still wasn't sure Liam knew…

Amy returned to peeling the potatoes. 'Will there be two or three for lunch?' she prompted lightly.

'Two! No—three. I don't know, Amy.' She sighed wearily. 'I'm not sure I know anything any more.'

Last night it had seemed so cut and dried: Liam was going to stay out of her personal life but continue to let Shipley publish his book. Liam turning up here this morning to play with Bobby made a nonsense of all that.

The housekeeper gave her a sympathetic smile. 'I know this isn't much comfort to you at the moment, but things do have a way of working themselves out.'

But not always as one would like them to!

Could Amy be right, that Liam did know Bobby was his son? And, if he did, why hadn't he challenged her about it?

She was no nearer knowing the workings of Liam's inner mind now than she had been eight years ago!

'I think I'll go out and say good morning,' she decided firmly, draining her coffee cup before standing up. 'That should be harmless enough.'

Amy nodded. 'And I'll prepare lunch for three. Just in case,' she added with a glint in her eyes.

Laura watched the two males in the garden unobserved for several minutes. Bobby was wrapped up warm in his winter coat; Liam was looking lithely attractive in denims and a thick blue chunky sweater.

Both faces were lit up with boyish pleasure as they gazed up at the red kite high in the sky above them, dark hair ruffled, blue eyes glowing. Bobby was holding on to the string but Liam was standing behind him, helping to guide the kite away from entanglement with neighbouring trees.

Laura felt an emotional pain in her chest as she watched them. How different their lives could have been if Liam hadn't walked out of her life eight years ago...

But by the same token, as Amy had already said this morning, if Liam hadn't gone Robert would never have enjoyed five years of family life.

Besides, what was the point of regretting something that was already a fact? Liam had left, and Robert had become her husband and Bobby's father. Nothing could ever change that.

'That looks like fun,' she called out to the two kite-flyers.

'Mummy!' Bobby cried excitedly, grinning from ear to ear as he looked at her. 'Look, Liam bought me a kite.'

Liam glanced over his shoulder at her, his expression slightly wary. And with good reason, Laura thought crossly, all her old resentment resurfacing at sight of him! Bringing her son presents, stopping to play with him, had not been part of their agreement the evening before.

Her gaze met Liam's questioningly. 'That's nice,' she said challengingly.

Liam met that gaze unflinchingly. 'Did you have a good sleep?' he enquired.

Almost as if he knew it had been the early hours of the morning before sleep finally claimed her! 'Very good, thank you,' she said tersely, going down the steps into the garden.

Liam watched her progress down the lawn as she walked towards them, his eyes narrowed on her slenderness in the black denims and deep blue jumper. She knew soft wisps of her dark hair were framing the paleness of her make-upless face.

Well, she hadn't realised they would have a visitor so early on a Sunday morning!

Laura met his gaze unflinchingly. 'Enjoying yourselves?' she asked.

'Isn't it great?' Bobby was the one to enthuse, obviously thrilled with his new toy, 'I've always wanted a kite of my own,' he explained with a grin looking up at Liam.

Laura felt that pain in her chest again as she looked at the two of them. How could they possibly have become so close in the hour or so Liam had been here? A natural gravitation to each other…? Whatever it was, that ache in her chest was starting to become a permanent feature!

'I trust you thanked Liam for his gift?' she asked Bobby, completely avoiding looking at Liam now.

Anyone looking at them, Laura knew, who was unaware of the real circumstances, would have assumed they were a family: mother and father with a much-loved son. But anyone would be wrong. Very wrong!

'Of course I did,' Bobby replied with obvious surprise; one thing he had known from an early age were good manners.

Her resentment at Liam's presence here was starting to show, even to Bobby, Laura realised guiltily. But how else was she supposed to feel? Liam should not be here!

'All little boys love to have a kite of their own to fly,' Liam chuckled.

But it felt like a slap in the face to her that Liam had been the one to realise—and rectify!—the lack of a kite in her son's life. It seemed to bring into glaring focus her own inadequacies as a single mother, concerning the upbringing of the little boy. A father would have realised about the kite. Robert, for all he had lacked experience in the role until the late arrival of Bobby into his life, would have realised.

Laura couldn't help wondering what other oversights, as a lone female bringing up a male, she might have made…

'Don't start beating yourself with a stick,' Liam said softly at her side, his gaze soft on her face now as Bobby moved off down the garden, holding tightly to the string of his kite. 'I would be just as lost if you happened to have a daughter rather than a son,' he assured her.

Laura looked up at him. 'That situation will never arise,' she told him distantly.

Dark brows rose over mocking blue eyes. 'You aren't even thirty yet, Laura!'

Old enough to know she would never have any more children. After her earlier mistake she knew she would have to be married for that to happen.

The only man she had ever loved in a romantic way had walked out of her life without even a glance backwards. The man she had married, although she hadn't loved him in the same way, had been the most wonderful man she could ever hope to meet. To expect she could ever find both those things in another man was just expecting too much…

'Old enough to know better,' she retorted.

Liam seemed to have lost interest in the subject as he turned his attention back to Bobby.

At least, it seemed that he had until his next remark.

'Would you have married me, Laura, if I had asked you eight years ago?'

Laura gasped at the unexpectedness of the question, all the colour draining from her cheeks as she looked up at him with widely hurt eyes.

She had told Amy that Liam had never asked her to marry him, but would she have married Liam eight years ago if he had?

Like a shot came the instant answer. She had lived for him eight years ago, would have done anything for him. *Had* done anything for him. If he had asked her to marry him she would have become his slave for life!

She breathed deeply and evenly, desperately trying to regain control over her shattered composure. He had no right! No right at all to say things like this to her!

'I was very naïve and inexperienced, Liam,' she finally answered.

'That's no answer, Laura,' he responded. 'Besides, you assured me—only yesterday, wasn't it…?—that where I was concerned you were never a child.'

'It's possible to be naïve and inexperienced at any age, Liam,' she came back. 'But to answer your question…' She drew in a sharp breath. 'I suppose it would have to be yes,' she bit out with distaste. 'And what a pretty mess that would have made of both our lives!'

Liam looked down at her searchingly. 'Do you really believe that?' he finally asked.

She gave him a pitying look. 'Don't you?' she derided. 'Liam, I meant so much to you then that you were married to someone else within weeks of leaving England—'

'A mistake I definitely wouldn't have made if I had already been married to you!' He reached out to grasp the tops of her arms. 'You might just have been what I needed to keep my feet on the ground!'

Laura shook her head ruefully. 'And I might just have got myself trampled to death in your stampede to get out of any marriage between the two of us!'

Liam gave a perplexed frown, shaking his head. 'You don't regret a thing, do you...?' he realised slowly, his hands dropping away from her arms.

In a word—no. If she had never been involved with Liam then she could never have given Robert, a man she had already owed so much, the family he had so desired. Her marriage to Robert was something she would never regret. If she regretted anything at all, then it was meeting Liam again—

Was it?

Did she really wish that had never happened?

She looked up at him searchingly, at the changes in him, the obvious signs of physical maturity. But hadn't he changed in other ways too? Hadn't he shown concern for her yesterday morning over that newspaper article? An article he was completely responsible for, though, she acknowledged hardly. But he could have had no idea of how far Janey Wilson would play up the possibility of a personal relationship between the two of them.

More to the point, much as she might like to try to deny it, even to herself, hadn't she responded to Liam yesterday morning? Hadn't she forgotten everything but the two of them, totally lost in the aching need, the long forgotten emotions Liam had roused in her? What would have been the conclusion of that meeting if Bobby hadn't interrupted them?

She swallowed hard, her eyes meeting Liam's unwaveringly. 'There's no point in regrets, Liam,' she told him flatly. 'The past is gone, never to return. The future is unknown, for all of us. Which only leaves the present. I'm quite happy with my present exactly the way that it is.' She looked across at Bobby, her eyes shining with pride.

'Then you must be one of the lucky ones,' Liam rasped. 'Because I don't like any of my life!'

Laura turned back to him slowly. 'Then do something about it.'

His face darkened angrily. 'I'm trying to! I—'

'Uncle Liam, the string's got caught in the tree!' Bobby's distressed wail interrupted them.

'"Uncle" Liam...?' Laura repeated with soft fury, her hand tightly on his arm, holding him back as he would have gone to her son's aid.

Liam turned back to her impatiently. 'He didn't know what else to call me.'

'*Uncle* Liam...?' she bit out furiously, annoyed beyond reason by the intimacy of the title.

'Come on, Laura.' Liam shook off her hold on his arm. 'He's a polite child. He didn't feel comfortable calling an adult by their first name. I couldn't see any harm in the title of uncle.'

'I'm sure you couldn't,' she replied. 'I happen to feel differently—'

'Why?' Liam turned fully back to face her. 'I seem to remember you have an honorary uncle of your own...?'

Laura became very still, the anger draining out of her as quickly as it had risen. She didn't want to talk about her own 'uncle'—!

'Where is he, by the way?' Liam continued scornfully.

'I've been here several times now, and he hasn't been in evidence once. Which is surprising, considering eight years ago you never stopped talking about the man! Don't tell me Mrs Shipley has become too high and mighty to bother with her beloved uncle any more?'

Laura was very pale now, her throat moving convulsively. 'Stop this, Liam,' she choked. 'Stop it now!'

'Why?' he challenged. 'What is it, Laura? Don't you like being reminded of your more humble beginnings?'

She swallowed hard. 'You don't know what you're talking about.'

'I know that you hurt me just now by your obvious aversion to having your son call me uncle—'

'And that gives you the right to hurt me in return?' She looked up at him with tear-wet eyes. 'You have no rights here, Liam, no rights at all, and—'

'Uncle Liam!' Bobby was becoming increasingly distressed at the sight of his kite entangled in the branches of the tree.

Laura glanced across at her son. 'You had better go and help him,' she said flatly. 'And then I would like you to leave.'

'And what you want you always get?' Liam countered.

'Almost never.' She shook her head sadly. 'Go and help Bobby,' she said dully, turning on her heel to walk back into the house.

Too close. Liam was getting far, far too close.

To everything…

But especially to the truth!

CHAPTER ELEVEN

'SO NICE of you to join us.' The sarcasm in Liam's tone was unmistakable as he looked across the restaurant table at Laura.

The meeting this morning between Liam and Perry had gone very well, and the two men had decided to go out to lunch to celebrate the settling of the deal and the signing of the contract. For reasons of her own, Laura had decided to join them.

The true fact of the matter was that after yesterday morning she didn't dare leave Liam alone socially with anyone who knew her! He was arrogant enough to question Perry about her personal life. Not too openly, of course, but she knew Liam well enough to realise he would find out what he wanted to know without Perry even realising he had given him the information.

Liam had done as she'd asked yesterday morning, and left as soon as he had finished flying the kite with Bobby. But, as Laura now knew only too well, his acquiescence counted for nothing; Liam would do exactly as he wanted when he wanted!

She shrugged dismissively. 'It's always nice to personally welcome a new author into the company.'

Liam smiled without humour. 'Even this one?'

'We're all really excited at welcoming you on board.' Perry was the one to answer him enthusiastically. 'You have a sure-fire number one bestseller in *Josie's World*, Liam.'

Liam raised dark brows. 'Now he tells me,' he drawled

mockingly. 'Is that your considered opinion too, Laura?' he prompted, his guarded gaze giving away none of his inner feelings.

Considered opinion…? She wasn't sure she had those any more! 'It's going to do very well for you,' she told him non-committally.

'And Shipley Publishing,' he pointed out.

She shrugged again. 'It would be madness to allow a bestseller to slip through our fingers; so many publishing companies are in financial difficulties nowadays.'

'But not Shipley,' Liam said with certainty. 'I checked before sending in the manuscript.'

'And decided to hitch your star to a winner?' Laura returned sharply.

His mouth twisted scornfully. 'It seems we have more in common than we realised.'

Colour brightened Laura's cheeks. So Liam was back to implying that she had married Robert for his position and money! Well, even that was probably preferable to him learning the truth…!

Perry, Laura saw with some dismay, was listening to the exchange with a slightly puzzled look on his face.

And no wonder; the antagonism between Liam and herself was tangible, seemed to fill the very air about their luncheon table!

She sat forward with deliberation, lifting the glass of champagne that had been poured for her minutes earlier, encouraging the two men to do the same. 'Success,' she toasted.

'I'll certainly drink to that!' Perry touched his glass lightly to hers before turning to do the same with Liam's.

'And a peaceful life,' Liam added as he touched his glass against the side of Laura's.

'Do the two go together?' she came back sceptically.

Another photograph of Liam and herself, as Liam had arrived at her house on Sunday morning, had appeared in the newspapers today. Laura had taken one glance at the photograph before throwing the newspaper in the bin. As she had warned Liam at the time, the situation was out of his control now.

He nodded grimly. 'If you want it badly enough, yes.'

'I hope you're right,' Laura returned dryly.

There had been more reporters camped out outside her home this morning. Disappointed reporters as they'd seen she was alone in the back of the car with Bobby, on her way to dropping him off at school before continuing on to her office. Her son, at least, seemed to have suffered no ill-effects from the last few days!

'I'm returning to Ireland tomorrow,' Liam put in. 'Can I come and see Bobby before I leave?'

Laura gave him a sharp look, aware of Perry's quiet interest in the conversation. No doubt he had seen those photographs in the newspapers too!

Her own relief at Liam's first statement had definitely been ruined by his second!

'I don't want Bobby to think I've just disappeared out of his life,' Liam continued.

Why not? He had just disappeared out of her own life eight years ago!

'You have changed,' she replied.

Liam's gaze was glacial as it met her challenging one across the width of the table.

'Shall we order?' Perry prompted lightly as a waiter appeared beside their table.

Laura felt as if food would choke her! But she had to stay here and eat her lunch without making a scene. Besides, her reason for being here in the first place still existed…

'You didn't answer my question?' Liam persisted once their order had been taken.

She took another sip of her champagne. She didn't want Liam anywhere near Bobby. Didn't want him anywhere near either of them, come to think of it!

'On condition you don't stay too long,' she finally answered. 'It's a school day, and Bobby has homework to do before bedtime,' she added in explanation—resentful at having to make one at all! She owed this man no explanations. About anything!

Liam gave an abrupt inclination of his head. 'I'll try not to interfere with that.'

He might try. But, as Laura knew only too well, he was unlikely to succeed; Bobby had taken an extreme liking to the man he called 'Uncle Liam', had talked of little else after Liam had left yesterday. Much to Laura's dismay. Bobby would be very reluctant to let Liam leave again once at the house.

Lunch was a stilted affair, despite Perry's many attempts to lighten the atmosphere, and Laura, for one, was more than glad when it was finally over. She had eaten little anyway, drunk several glasses of champagne instead, and her head felt more than a little light.

'Steady.' Liam grasped her elbow as they went outside, the fresh air seeming to have a dizzying effect on her. 'You really should eat more, Laura,' he admonished, keeping a firm hold of her as he guided her over the road to where Paul had parked the car, holding the door open as he waited for her.

'When I want your opinion I'll ask for it,' Laura snapped back, her irritability audible only to Liam as she settled into the back of the car. Perry had gone round to the other door and was now seated beside her. 'Can we drop you anywhere?' Preferably on his head, she thought childishly!

She had drunk too much! Which was most unlike her; she had never been a big drinker, and since Bobby was born, when she had needed to be mentally alert twenty-four hours a day, she had only ever drunk the occasional glass of white wine with a meal. Three glasses of champagne at lunchtime was definitely out of character. It would be a relief—to her, at least!—when Liam returned to Ireland!

Liam's expression changed, almost as if he were able to read her thoughts and was amused by them. 'No, thanks, the walk will do me good. Is five-thirty okay for calling in to see Bobby?'

Perfect; as they always dined at six in the week, she would have a good excuse for asking him to leave. Unless Bobby, in his youthful enthusiasm, decided to invite his new friend to stay to dinner with them…?

'That's absolutely fine,' she agreed firmly. 'That way I'll be able to sit down and do Bobby's homework with him before we have dinner at six.' She couldn't say any clearer than that that Liam wasn't invited to join them for the meal without being extremely rude—and only Perry's presence stopped her being exactly that!

Blue eyes glittered with hard amusement before Liam turned to smile at Perry. 'I'll call you when I intend coming back to London.'

Laura kept her face averted as the car door was finally closed. Paul manoeuvred the car out into the early-afternoon traffic, her sigh of relief as he did so audible only to herself. She hoped.

'Well, that went off better than expected, don't you think?' she said lightly to Perry.

'I'm not sure what I expected,' Perry answered slowly. 'You and Liam are obviously old friends, but—'

'I was referring to the business aspect of the meeting,' Laura put in quickly.

'Oh, that.' Perry nodded his satisfaction. 'Yes, that went very well.'

Laura turned to him, her brows raised. 'But…?'

Her senior editor hesitated. 'Maybe there isn't a but.' He grimaced. 'I just have the feeling that—well, that—'

'Yes?'

'I think it's a good idea that you persuaded Liam to accept me as his editor—'

'*I* persuaded him?'

'Well, didn't you?' Perry said.

She had completely lost track of who had persuaded who to do what! She did know that she still felt she had been manoeuvred into this situation by Liam. And she probably had!

'Not that I recall, Perry,' she said dully. 'Although I do approve of the arrangement.'

He nodded. 'It isn't a good idea to mix business with pleasure.'

Pleasure? With Liam? The man had been nothing but a thorn in her side from the moment she'd met him again!

'I think you've misunderstood the situation between Liam and myself, Perry,' she answered evenly.

'Hey, I wasn't criticising,' he instantly assured her. 'I have no right to do that, anyway. However, if you don't mind my saying so, it's good to see you have someone in your life again. You've been on your own too long, Laura.'

She *did* mind him saying so! But with those wretched photographs in the newspapers, and Liam's request to call at the house later this evening, she was only going to make the situation worse if she protested too much.

Perry's remarks did not put her in a particularly good humour for welcoming Liam into her home later that evening. She scowled at him as Amy showed him into the sitting room, where Laura stood alone beside the unlit fireplace. Bobby was upstairs changing in anticipation of Liam's arrival.

'Champagne worn off?' Liam queried once they were alone, as he took in her glowering expression.

The fact that that could be half the reason she felt so irritable did not elevate her mood one little bit! 'How like you to pass the blame on to something other than yourself,' she snapped scathingly. She was still wearing the black suit and cream blouse she had worn to work today, very conscious of Perry's comments concerning business and pleasure; she wanted to make it clear that for her part this association with Liam was solely business!

Liam's own expression darkened. 'You really should try to put your bitterness behind you, Laura,' he advised. 'After all, you did all right for yourself in my absence.' He looked about them pointedly at the obviously luxurious comfort of her home.

Angry colour darkened her cheeks at his obvious accusation. 'Making snide remarks about me isn't going to change the fact that you deserted me eight years ago—'

'Deserted you?' Liam repeated in a steely voice. 'Isn't that rather an odd way of putting it…?'

It was the way she had thought of Liam's departure for so long. But that didn't change the fact that it must sound odd to someone who didn't know all the circumstances…

'Perhaps,' she conceded non-committally. 'It isn't important, anyway—'

'I happen to think it is,' Liam interrupted. 'You—'

'Uncle Liam!' An ecstatic Bobby burst into the room, launching himself at Liam.

Liam picked him up under his arms and swung him round. 'Hello, *spalpeen*.' He grinned up at Bobby as he held him high.

'Spalpeen?' Bobby repeated with a puzzled frown.

'Rascal,' Liam translated lightly, putting Bobby back on the ground. 'Had a good day at school?' He ruffled the darkness of Bobby's hair.

'It was okay,' the little boy replied. 'Can we go outside and fly my kite again?'

'I'm not sure… I can't stay long, Bobby,' Liam added gently, after a brief glance at Laura. 'I have an early-morning flight back to Ireland tomorrow,' he explained softly.

Laura hadn't told Bobby the reason for Liam's visit this evening, had felt it would be best coming from Liam himself. From the look of tearful disappointment on her son's face maybe she should have spoken to her son first.

'Bobby—'

'When will you be back?' Bobby completely ignored Laura's soothing tone, staring intently up at Liam.

Liam's expression softened as he went down on his haunches beside the little boy. 'A few weeks, possibly,' he answered, reaching out to touch Bobby's arm.

Laura watched in dismay as her son wrenched away from Liam, his face dark with rebellion.

'You won't! I know you won't!' Bobby was rigid with resentment, blue eyes sparkling angrily.

Laura could only stare at her son; she had never seen him behave in this way before. She knew he had grown fond of Liam the last few days, but this was completely unexpected.

Liam glanced up at her, frowning darkly. 'Of course I'll be back, Bobby. And when I do—'

'You'll never come back,' Bobby cried, shaking his head, his face flushed with emotion. 'My daddy went away and he never came back!' He was breathing hard in his agitation.

Laura swallowed hard, feeling tears sting her eyes.

'Bobby, this isn't the same at all.' She made a move towards him, only to come to a halt as he began to back away from her towards the door. 'Daddy was ill, Bobby. You know that,' she told him huskily. 'He didn't want to go away. He just didn't have any choice,' she said emotionally.

'Liam has a choice—and he's still going away!' Bobby accused stubbornly, glaring at Liam now. 'I thought you liked me,' he declared chokingly.

Liam had straightened, frowning his consternation at Bobby's reaction. 'I do like you, Bobby. I'll only be gone for a short time, I promise you—'

'No.' Bobby was shaking his head in disbelief, his hand on the doorhandle now. 'Take your old kite with you! I don't want it any more!' came his parting shot as he wrenched open the door. The sound of his feet running up the stairs could be heard seconds later.

Laura was stunned. Shocked. Dismayed.

Where had all that come from?

She had spent hours with Bobby after Robert's death, explaining about his father's illness, how Robert hadn't wanted to leave them, that his heart had just given up under the strain. From Bobby's outburst just now she felt she couldn't have got through to him at all.

She dropped down heavily into one of the armchairs before her shaking legs refused to hold her up any more. 'I—' She swallowed hard, holding a hand up to her stricken face as her lips began to tremble. 'Oh…!' She buried her face in her hands as the tears began to fall.

This was too much, just too much, after the strain of the last few days!

'Laura!' Liam came to sit on the arm of her chair, gathering her up into his arms, holding her tightly against his chest. 'Bobby didn't mean any of that, you know,' he soothed, after letting her cry for several minutes. 'He's just hurting right now, hitting out.'

She shook her head. 'I had no idea he felt abandoned after Robert's death. I—I thought he understood.' She sighed shakily. 'I must go to him.'

Liam's arms tightened about her as she would have got up. 'Leave him for a few minutes,' he advised. 'At the moment he's so angry, at both of us, that he might say something in the heat of the moment that he will bitterly regret.' Liam looked down at her ruefully. 'One thing's for sure, your decision concerning transient friends in your life seems to have been the right one!'

Laura felt a jolt in her chest. Transient friend? Was that what Liam was?

'No, it isn't,' Liam firmly answered her unasked question. 'You know that isn't what I want at all.'

Did she? Not really. Liam had shown her—all too clearly!—that he would like to resume some sort of relationship with her, but she had no idea what he had in mind!

He was right about one thing: she had been right to try and protect Bobby from being hurt again by coming to care for a man who was simply going to walk out of his life when he felt like it...

Although until the last few minutes she had been completely unaware of how Bobby felt deserted by Robert.

'I really must go up to him,' she said firmly, releasing herself from Liam's arms to stand up, smoothing down the shortness of her hair before turning back to him. 'I think it might be better if you had already left when Bobby comes back downstairs.'

Liam looked up at her searchingly. 'I will be coming back, you know, Laura,' he told her.

Her mouth quirked humourlessly. 'Well, I suppose that

possibility is more than you gave me eight years ago,' she said bitterly.

His expression tightened, his eyes flashing deeply blue. 'Is it…?'

She eyed him warily. 'Isn't it?' she challenged defensively.

He stood up abruptly. 'I have some business to attend to in Ireland—'

'Business, Liam?' she echoed tauntingly. 'Would that be business of the female kind?'

He drew in a harsh breath at her deliberately insulting tone. 'I realise you're upset at the moment, Laura.' Otherwise she wouldn't be getting away with this so easily, his own tone implied! 'And as it happens, yes, it's of the "female kind"; it's my mother's sixtieth birthday on Wednesday. We're having a surprise family party for her. Obviously I have to be there,' he added dryly.

'Obviously,' Laura echoed, wondering how Mary O'Reilly would react if presented with the biggest surprise in her life: her grandson, Bobby!

'You could always come with me.'

She looked up at Liam sharply, wondering if her own thoughts could possibly have been reflected on her face. Liam steadily returned her searching gaze, giving away none of his own thoughts.

'And Bobby, of course.'

'I don't think so, thank you,' Laura replied dismissively, her hands clenched so tightly at her sides her fingernails were digging painfully into the palms. 'As you said, it's a family party.' She looked across at him challengingly.

'As I said…' He gave an acknowledging inclination of his head. 'In view of Bobby's upset, I'll be coming back on Thursday, Laura. And when I get back I think we need to talk. I mean really talk.'

'I—'

'Don't you?' he queried pointedly.

No, she didn't! But if she knew anything about Liam—and she knew a great deal!—she knew she wouldn't have much choice in the matter!

Did he know Bobby was his son? Did he know, one hundred percent certain, that he was Bobby's father? And, if he did, why didn't he just come right out and say so?

Now was the perfect time for Liam to launch into his attack, when she was already feeling utterly defeated by Bobby's emotional outburst. So why didn't he...?

Liam shook his head as he watched the emotions flickering across her face. 'I'm not the man you thought I was eight years ago, Laura,' he told her. 'Then I tried to act noble—and ended up being completely the opposite! This time around I'm determined to succeed.'

'Noble?' Laura repeated dazedly; it wasn't a word she had ever associated with Liam! 'I don't know what you're talking about.'

'No, I know you don't.' He gave a humourless smile. 'But that's part of what we need to talk about. I'll get here on Thursday in time to speak to Bobby before he goes to bed; keep the rest of the evening free for me, Laura.'

She moistened dry lips. 'I—'

'Go up and talk to Bobby now,' he continued firmly. 'Tell him I'm coming back. And make him believe it,' he added grimly.

How could she be expected to do that when she wasn't sure she believed it herself...?

CHAPTER TWELVE

'FINISHED?' She looked questioningly at her son as he left half the pizza that she had ordered for him on his plate.

Since their talk on Monday evening Bobby had been very quiet. He had seemed to accept what she'd said about Robert, and why he had died, but at the same time had not quite believed what she'd said about Liam's intention of coming back today.

Maybe because she still wasn't sure she believed that herself…!

Liam had telephoned her from the airport on Tuesday morning before his plane took off, wanting to know how her talk with Bobby had gone. Not that she'd been able to reassure Liam too much on that point; Bobby just wasn't giving away his feelings at the moment.

Other than that brief telephone call from Liam she had heard nothing from him the last three days, had no idea whether or not he still intended coming to the house this evening. It was a point Bobby was well aware of; the first question he had asked when he'd woken up this morning was had she heard from Liam? Which she hadn't. And still hadn't, as the day progressed.

Which was one of the reasons she had decided to take Bobby out for a pizza after school, hoping to take his mind off Liam's proposed visit. Although, from Bobby's lack of appetite, she might as well not have bothered!

'Finished. Can we go home now?' he asked eagerly.

She gave a weak smile. 'Of course.' She stood up to pay the bill, feeling an ache in her chest at Bobby's obviously suppressed excitement; he was just too afraid to dare to outwardly anticipate that Liam would keep his promise.

Laura knew the feeling.

Only too well!

But this bewildered pain was exactly what she hadn't wanted for Bobby, was the reason she would have preferred Liam and Bobby never to meet. Of course, she couldn't have anticipated the invisible bond that had come into existence between the two of them from the moment they had met, but she had known enough not to want even to take the risk of the two of them forming an attachment. Because it *was* a risk. To Bobby's fragile emotions...

But, after doing everything in her power to prevent the two of them ever meeting, she had bowed to the fact that they had, that there was nothing she could do about the fact they actually liked each other. What she would do was personally strangle Liam if he let Bobby down this evening!

Bobby could barely contain his excitement on the drive back to the house. Laura was relieved at having the concentration of driving herself, for a change, to keep her own mind from dwelling on the possibility of Liam's arrival. In fact, she had chosen to drive herself for that very reason.

Bobby waited barely long enough for her to bring the car to a halt in front of the house before jumping out and running in, leaving the front door wide open as he did so. Laura followed at a more leisurely pace, reluctant to feel the sting of her own disappointment as well as Bobby's.

'What kept you, Mrs Shipley?' drawled an achingly familiar voice as she entered the hallway.

She couldn't help it; her pulse rate quickened at the sound of Liam's voice, her eyes glowing with pleasure as she looked up at him standing only feet away with a grinning Bobby held up in his arms.

Her breath caught in her throat as she realised how right

they looked together. But it wasn't with that wariness she had felt from the moment she met Liam again over a week ago, this was something completely different…

She was still in love with Liam!

Had she ever stopped…?

She had thought she had, had believed, when she'd finally accepted Liam had left her eight years ago, that her love for him had died too. But looking at him now, so achingly familiar, his eyes smiling into hers, their son held in his arms, Laura knew that she had never stopped being in love with Liam, that she had only buried that emotion deep in her heart, never to be looked at again.

Except Liam was back…

'He came back, Mummy.' Bobby's words echoed her chaotic thoughts.

She swallowed hard, inwardly struggling to behave naturally, even if she did feel like screaming at the painful discovery she had just made. 'So he did,' she acknowledged lightly, concentrating on putting her bag down on the hall table so that she no longer had to look at Liam.

How could she have continued to love him all this time?

How could she not? came the next instant thought; every time she looked at Bobby, the son she loved above everyone and everything else in life, her love for Liam, the man he resembled so strongly, became more deeply entrenched in her heart.

'Okay, Laura?'

She looked up to find Liam looking at her concernedly. But how could everything be okay when she had just realised her love for this man?

She swallowed hard, avoiding that searching blue gaze. 'If you don't mind, I'll leave you two to chat while I go up and change.'

Liam continued to look at her frowningly for several long

seconds before giving a barely perceptible shrug. 'Don't be long; I've brought you back a piece of my mother's birthday cake.'

Wonderful—it would probably choke her!

She fled up the stairs, throwing herself dazedly down on her bed once she reached her room. She was still in love with Liam! Unbelievable. Incredible. Impossible!

Oh, Liam had made it more than obvious that he still found her attractive, that he would be happy for the two of them to have some sort of relationship. But too much had happened in the last eight years, to both of them, for them ever to be able to start all over again.

Besides, there was still Bobby…

Bobby was Liam's son, as well as her own. When Liam had left her life so suddenly eight years ago…had married another woman within weeks of leaving…Laura had known, once she found out, that she couldn't contact him to tell him she was pregnant; she simply hadn't wanted him in her life, in any guise, under those terms.

But what of Bobby's life? Her decision had meant that neither Bobby or Liam knew of the other's existence.

There was no doubting that Robert had been a wonderful father to Bobby, but, given a choice, would Bobby rather have had his own father, even on a part-time basis? More to the point, how would Liam see, in the light of his unknowing absence in America, what she had chosen to do eight years ago?

He should never have left her in the way he had!

This wasn't solving anything, she acknowledged heavily. She might still be angry with Liam for deserting her in the way that he had, but Liam might be just as angry with her at not being told of her pregnancy. Hadn't he made a comment last week along the lines of not having made the mistakes in his own life over the last eight years if she had been his wife when he went to America...?

Laura sighed heavily, having no idea what she was going to do now. She was in love with the father of her son. Under other circumstances it would be the most natural way in the world for her to feel. Under these particular circumstances, it might be just as disastrous for her as loving Liam eight years ago had been.

What was she going to do?

Liam had told her that they needed to talk this evening, once Bobby had gone to bed. She was starting to dread what that conversation might be about!

'Come and have some cake, Mummy,' Bobby invited as soon as she entered the kitchen. A pot of coffee, and a plate of cake, were laid out on the wooden table. 'It's delicious!'

'One of my sisters made it,' Liam supplied, his expression indulgent as he watched Bobby enjoying his slice of cake. The little boy's appetite had obviously returned.

'Domesticity has never been my forte,' Laura heard herself snap in reply, instantly cringing inwardly. It wasn't Liam's sister's fault Laura had just discovered she was still in love with him!

Liam raised dark brows at her sharpness. 'Tough day?' he sympathised.

Laura felt the sting of tears in her eyes at the gentleness of his tone. The last thing she could cope with right now was Liam being kind to her! Especially when she had just so obviously been a bitch.

She gave an uninterested shrug, having changed into denims and a loose blue jumper. 'No tougher than usual. Where's Amy?' She frowned at the absence of her housekeeper.

'She said to tell you she had to pop out for a couple of things,' Liam explained, still frowning slightly.

Probably because Laura had forgotten to mention to Amy there was a possibility of Liam being here for dinner this evening! Because she hadn't wanted to end up looking a fool when he didn't arrive.

'You're looking tired, Laura.' Liam looked at her concernedly. 'Do you have to work so hard?'

Her eyes flashed her resentment as she glared across the room at him. 'I have a business to run!'

He nodded slowly. 'And a child to look after and a home,' he elaborated.

None of those things were the reason she looked so tired; the truth of the matter was she hadn't slept well since Liam had left on Monday evening. And she hadn't even realised she was still in love with him then!

'Liam, in this day and age lots of women have a bigger workload to cope with than I do,' she replied.

'But probably not as much lone responsibility,' he persisted. 'From what I've observed you're a working single mother, and Shipley's is a big company to run—'

'The art department have started work on the cover of your book, by the way,' she interrupted brightly. 'I think you'll be pleased with it.'

'I'm sure I will,' he dismissed uninterestedly. 'Come and sit down, Laura, and I'll pour you a cup of coffee.'

Laura sat. Not because Liam had told her to, but because she was still deeply shaken by the realisation she was in love with him.

Bobby, she could see at a glance, looked happier than he had in days. Obviously because of Liam's presence. What was she going to *do*?

'Stop worrying so much,' Liam murmured at her side, reaching out to briefly squeeze her hand with his. 'Things will work out.'

Would they? Would they really? Somehow she didn't

feel that Liam would still feel that way once he learnt the truth. And a part of her said she now owed him and Bobby that, at least…

It was at times like this that she wished she had an older sister she could talk to, or a close friend she could confide in. But, as Liam had already pointed out, her life was kept busy enough being Bobby's mother and running Shipley Publishing. The closest she came to having a female friend was Amy, and because Amy had worked for over twenty years for Robert Laura knew she would feel slightly disloyal talking to the other woman about her feelings for Liam.

'I'll go upstairs to my room and get my kite,' Bobby said excitedly, having devoured two slices of birthday cake.

Laura watched her son leave the room, all the time wishing that he hadn't. She had no idea what she was going to say to Liam now that they were alone.

She sipped her coffee, warming her hands around the cup; for some reason she felt incredibly cold. 'Did you have a nice time with your family in Ireland?' She tried to pick an innocuous subject to talk about; they had hours to get through before Bobby went to bed and the two of them could have that talk.

'I missed you and Bobby,' Liam came back—instantly turning the conversation back into intimacy.

Laura looked down at the table-top, wondering how she was going to get through this without breaking down.

'I'm sure your family were pleased to see you,' she said. 'Was your mother suitably surprised with her party?'

'She appeared to be.' Liam smiled indulgently. 'Although I'm sure she knew exactly what was going on. My mother is a woman who sees a great deal that isn't actually said,' he replied appreciatively. 'She saw the photographs of the two of us in the newspapers,' he added gruffly.

Laura winced. Oh, no, she hadn't given a thought to the fact Liam's family might see them too. And wonder… 'Did your family give you a hard time over them?' she attempted to tease.

He shrugged broad shoulders, having discarded his outer coat, wearing a black shirt and blue denims. 'Not particularly. I think my mother took one look at me and warned them off the subject. She would like to meet you,' he added gently.

Laura took in a hard breath. 'Didn't you explain to her that those stories in the newspapers were just publicity nonsense dreamed up by the reporters?'

Liam's mouth quirked into a smile. 'There would have been no point; my mother has always been able to tell when I'm lying!'

Laura raised startled lids, those different coloured eyes, one blue and one green, shining brightly with confusion.

Liam shrugged. 'Of course, she doesn't realise you're the same Laura from eight years ago yet, but—'

'Your mother knew about me then?' Laura gasped, her eyes wide.

'Oh, yes, she knew.' He nodded slowly.

'But—'

'Here we are.' A happy Bobby bounced back into the room with his kite. 'Can Liam and I go outside for a while Mummy?'

Almost as if Liam were Bobby's own age, and the two of them were going out to play in the garden!

'If Liam wants to,' she answered non-committally.

Liam stood up, grinning. 'I've thought of doing nothing else the last three days!'

Somehow Laura found that hard to believe, but if it made Bobby happy—which it most assuredly did, as his face lit with excitement when he and Liam went outside—then who was she to question the statement?

Besides, she was glad of this brief respite. Too much seemed to be happening too soon. And once Liam learnt how she had deceived him about Robert and Bobby it might just be going nowhere!

Liam had told his mother about her eight years ago…

Laura found that incredible. Admittedly their relationship had lasted over six months, but for most of that time Liam had treated her like another one of his sisters—someone to be patted on the head when she did something right, or shouted at when she did something wrong.

Why on earth would Liam have told his mother about her?

Yet another fact from the past that needed explaining. By the time the two of them had finished explaining themselves, there would be nothing left!

'That was absolutely delicious, Amy,' Liam told the housekeeper warmly as she took away their used plates before putting cheese and a pot of coffee on the table.

'Thank you, Mr O'Reilly,' Amy accepted before turning to Laura. 'I'll clear away in the kitchen, check on Bobby, and then call it a night, if that's okay with you, Mrs Shipley?'

It wasn't okay with her, it meant she would be left on her own with Liam, but, like her, Amy had had a long and tiring day and deserved some time to herself.

Bobby had been bathed and in bed for over an hour now, having insisted Liam join them for his story. Just as if they were a real family, Laura had realised. This situation was definitely getting out of hand!

And maybe the sooner it was settled—in whatever way!—the better it would be for all of them.

Nevertheless, Laura felt her stomach give a nervous lurch as Amy closed the dining room door softly behind her as she left.

'You should know me well enough by now, Laura, to know that I don't bite!'

She looked up at Liam, instantly looking away again as she saw from his teasing expression that he had meant the remark in a double-edged way; he wasn't about to verbally attack her just because they were now alone, but at the same time he was reminding her of the fact that he had been a passionate but gentle lover eight years ago…!

'It never occurred to me to think you might,' she lied—having no idea how the rest of this evening was going to go!

'No?' he mocked lightly. 'I don't know about you, but I don't care for any cheese… Shall we take the coffee through to the sitting room, then?' he suggested after she confirmed she wanted nothing else to eat either.

Why not? It might only delay the dreaded moment for a couple of minutes, but it would delay it…

Liam didn't sit down once they were ensconced in the sitting room, but prowled around the room, as if he were reluctant to begin this conversation too.

He came to a halt beside the dresser at the back of the room, lifting one of the many photographs from its surface, looking down to study the picture intently.

Laura squeezed her eyes shut, knowing exactly which photograph he was looking at; it had been taken shortly after Bobby was born. Laura was sitting on the arm of one of the chairs in this room, Robert was seated in the chair and Bobby nestled contentedly in his arms.

'You look a happy family.' Liam spoke gruffly.

Laura opened her eyes to look across at him, but found

herself unable to read anything from Liam's closed expression. 'We were,' she confirmed quietly.

Liam gave an abrupt inclination of his head. 'Robert was a good father?'

She swallowed hard. 'He was,' she confirmed, aware they were both talking around the real point at issue. But at least they were talking.

'And a good husband?'

Her head rose challengingly. 'I've already told you that he was,' she answered.

Liam nodded slowly, replacing the photograph. 'I'm glad.'

Her eyes widened. 'You are?'

His gaze was shuttered as he gave her a considering look. 'Didn't you think I would be?'

Laura shook her head. 'I don't know,' she told him truthfully.

He gave a rueful smile. 'I've never wished you anything but happiness, Laura. Never. Do you believe me?'

How could she? He had become the sole reason for her happiness eight years ago, and six months later he had cruelly walked out of her life!

'Obviously not,' Liam acknowledged at her silence. 'Laura, eight years ago you were still a child—'

'I was over twenty-one,' she protested.

'Sixteen going on twenty-one,' Liam corrected softly. 'When your parents died they left you in an emotional time-warp of the age you were when they died—'

'That's utter nonsense, Liam, and you know it,' Laura declared.

'No, I don't?' He gave a firm shake of his head. 'Sixteen is a terrible age to lose both your parents. Admittedly you had a guardian who could take over the financial side of your life, but emotionally you had been left in wilderness.'

He gave another shake of his head. 'I had no idea of any of this when I first met you; how could I? But it rapidly became obvious to me that you were badly in need of someone to love. And for someone to love you.'

'And that wasn't part of your immediate plans, was it?'

'Laura,' he began patiently, 'you have no idea how I felt eight years ago. You weren't mature enough—'

'Oh, please!' She stood up impatiently. 'Don't try and blame any of what happened then on my so-called immaturity. I didn't see that stopping you when you made love to me!'

Liam drew in a harsh breath. 'Nothing could have stopped me the night—that one and only night!—I made love to you,' he admitted 'You had been in my life, every part of it, for almost six months. There, with your sensual allure, your undoubted beauty, your complete acceptance of who and what I was. Once I began to touch you that night, kiss you, I could no more have stopped either of those things than I could have stopped breathing!'

'You said it had been a mistake.' Laura shakily recalled his words of rejection the following morning. 'That it must never happen again.'

And it hadn't. It hadn't needed to. Bobby had been conceived from that single night of physical love between Liam and herself.

And Liam had left her life before she had even had a chance to share that knowledge with him…

'Obviously you'd had what you wanted, found it unsatisfactory, and simply moved on,' she bit out caustically, the words cutting into her like knives.

Liam's expression was dark with anger. 'Obviously you don't know a thing about how I felt after that night!' he shot back.

She eyed him scathingly. 'Triumphant, I expect.'

Liam stepped forward, grasping the tops of her arms. 'You were a virgin until that night, Laura. And I—I had taken that precious gift from you. Triumph didn't even enter into how I felt the next morning when I woke to find you beside me in my bed!'

Laura closed her eyes against the fury of Liam's face.

They had been out to celebrate that evening, Liam having signed the contract that day to go to Los Angeles and write the screenplay of his book. They had drunk too much champagne, already high enough on Liam's success. It had seemed the most natural thing in the world that the two of them should make love with each other when they returned to Liam's apartment. At least, it had seemed natural to Laura…

'I should never have drunk as much champagne as I did.' He scowled.

She opened her eyes to look up at him frowningly. 'What happened between us had nothing to do with the champagne.' She shook her head protestingly. 'It was always going to happen. I'm just surprised it took as long as it did,' she added, knowing she had fallen in love with Liam, had wanted him physically, from their second time of meeting. Liam had always been the one who held back.

Was this way? Had he really believed her too young and vulnerable to know what she was doing?

Liam's expression was grim as he thrust her away from him. 'It wasn't supposed to happen. I had told myself it wasn't going to. I was too old for you—'

'You're only ten years older than me, Liam, not Methuselah,' she said, her arms tingling where he had held her so tightly.

'In terms of experience I was totally out of line continuing my friendship with you at all!' he told her grimly. 'And I don't just mean physical experience,' he added at her derisive expression. 'I left Ireland when I was nineteen, came to live in London, found success with my writing. Those years before I met you I lived my life to the full. In every way.'

'And then stupidly naïve me came into your life,' Laura realised. 'Following you everywhere. Worming my way into every part of your life.'

'It wasn't like that at all, and you know it.' His eyes glittered dangerously. 'I liked having you there, came to look forward to the time we spent together. Too much! Because I was aware that you already had a blinkered adoration for your guardian, the man who had come to your rescue when you were left alone in the world. I also knew that I was rapidly taking on that same untouchable role in your eyes, of someone you thought could do no wrong—'

'Liam, that is utter nonsense,' Laura cut in incredulously.

'I was far from perfect,' he said.

Laura frowned. 'How I felt about you bore no relation to how I felt about—my guardian,' she said awkwardly. 'Yes, I adored him. How could I not? I had known him all my life; he was a friend of my parents. I told you he had always been an honorary uncle,' she added exasperatedly as Liam continued to look unconvinced.

'I know I learnt to be jealous of the man; you talked about him incessantly,' Liam said. 'Uncle Rob this and Uncle Rob that.'

'I loved him!' she cried exasperately. 'He was the kindest, most wonderful man I've…' Her voice trailed off as she saw Liam look at her sharply, a dawning recognition appearing in those intelligent blue eyes.

Liam swallowed hard. 'I seem to have heard that description somewhere before…' he said slowly.

Laura was flustered now, remembering all too well where

he had heard it before! The question was, was Liam remembering it too…?

He was breathing shallowly, his searching gaze never leaving the paleness of her face as he obviously tried to come to grips with a realisation that just seemed too incredible to take in.

'I've been a fool, haven't I?' He finally spoke slowly. 'A complete and utter damned fool.' His voice hardened angrily.

She hadn't meant him to find out like this, had wanted to explain the situation to him quietly and calmly. Unfortunately, those two things had never been too near the surface in her dealings with Liam!

'I can't believe how stupid I've been,' he continued self-disgustedly. 'I was just so bowled over when I met you again. I didn't connect— Guardian Uncle *Rob*. Husband *Robert*. They're one and the same person, aren't they?' he breathed incredulously.

Laura stared at him wordlessly, feeling the colour slowly drain from her face.

'Aren't they?' He moved swiftly, grasping her arms again. 'Answer me!'

His face was only inches away from her own, bombarding her with the full force of his anger.

She shook her head. 'You don't understand, Liam—'

'Robert Shipley was your guardian, wasn't he?' he ground out fiercely. 'The adored Uncle Rob you talked about all the time?'

'Yes!' she burst out forcefully, the tears beginning to fall hotly down her cheeks now.

Liam thrust her away from him, staring at her disbelievingly. 'I thought—believed— I've been making an idiot of myself, haven't I?' he exclaimed impatiently as he moved away.

'Where are you going?' she choked as he strode over to the door.

He looked back at her with glacial eyes. 'As far away from here as possible!'

'But—'

'Don't say another word, Laura,' Liam bit out in a dangerously controlled voice. 'Not another word. I won't be held responsible for the consequences if you do!'

She watched mutely as he swung the sitting room door back with a bang. The slam of the front door seconds later told her that he had gone. Never to return, probably.

And with that realisation came the knowledge that she still hadn't told him about Bobby, his son…!

CHAPTER THIRTEEN

SHE hadn't told him anything that mattered!

That, much as she had loved Robert, it hadn't been in the way she loved Liam. That Robert hadn't loved her in a romantic way either. That, as well as trying to help her once she had told him she was expecting Liam's baby, Robert had seen their marriage as a way of having the family he would never have had otherwise.

Liam had left before she could tell him any of that. Before she could explain.

She sat down, wondering what to do next. That Liam would never willingly come near her again she was certain. And he had to know the truth. No matter what the consequences, he had to finally know that. After the last few days she knew she owed that to Bobby as much as anyone else...

It didn't take long to organise herself—to check with the hotel Liam had stayed at previously and find that he had booked in there again earlier today, to knock on the door to Amy's flat and ask her to mind Bobby while she just popped out for a short time, to get her car out of the garage and drive to Liam's hotel. Before she lost her nerve!

That Liam would be reluctant to see her she didn't doubt. But he had to hear what she wanted to say. Not because she thought there was any chance left between the two of them, but because Bobby, without even knowing who Liam really was, had grown to love him. Her marriage seven and a half years ago had been to give Bobby a father, and, no matter what it cost her, she couldn't do less for him now.

'I believe I saw Mr O'Reilly go through to the bar a short time ago.' The pretty hotel receptionist answered her query brightly.

Laura was sure that if that was what this young lady believed, then it was true; Liam's attractiveness certainly hadn't dimmed over the years!

'Thank you.' She smiled distractedly, her steps reluctant as she walked towards the hotel bar. If Liam was drinking again…!

Do it, Laura, she told herself firmly. You came here to talk to him, and that's what you're going to do.

He sat alone in a corner booth of the dimly lit bar, a glass of what looked like whisky in front of him. Untouched whisky, if the high level in the glass was any indication.

Laura came to a halt beside his table, managing to remain unmoving as, sensing her presence, he looked up at her, his gaze instantly fiercely angry.

'What do you want?' he demanded unpleasantly, the lines about his eyes and mouth more pronounced.

What she really wanted was for him to sit there and listen while she talked, saying nothing in response to anything she said, and then for him to let her leave again!

'Can I join you?' she said quietly.

'Why not? It's a free country. Although there are plenty of empty tables if you just want a drink.'

'I don't.' She slid onto the bench-seat opposite his in the booth. 'You left earlier before I had finished talking,' she explained softly.

His gaze was scathing as he straightened, one hand reaching out, the fingers curling about the glass of whisky. 'Don't look so worried,' he derided as she gave a wary glance at the glass. 'I ordered this twenty minutes ago and

I haven't touched any of it yet!' But there's still time, his words seemed to imply!

Laura sighed heavily, shaking her head in the direction of the young barman as he came over to see if she would like a drink; she already knew she wasn't going to enjoy the next few minutes, and Dutch courage wasn't going to help!

She drew in a deep breath. 'Liam, there are—things about my marriage that you can't possibly be aware of,' she began carefully. 'Circumstances that—'

'Are we talking about Bobby?' he cut in harshly.

She swallowed hard. 'What about Bobby?'

'Maybe these will help,' Liam ground out, reaching into the breast pocket of his jacket to pull out several photographs. He placed them carefully, side by side, on the table in front of her.

Laura moved forward slowly, looking down at those photographs. Apart from the fact that the clothes were all wrong, dating the photographs at thirty years or so ago, the little boy smiling into the camera in all of them could have been Bobby!

'You?' she managed to croak.

'I asked my mother for them when I was in Ireland,' Liam confirmed, gathering up the photographs to put them back in the pocket of his jacket.

Laura moistened dry lips. 'How long have you known?'

'That you must have been pregnant when I left eight years ago?' Liam paused. 'From the first moment I set eyes on Bobby.'

Her eyes widened incredulously at the admission. 'Then why—?'

'Why didn't I say something?' Liam finished raggedly. 'I've been waiting for you to tell me! Again I was being stupid.'

'I was going to tell you—'

'When?' he demanded.

'Tonight. But before I could—'

'I realised that your husband had been your beloved Uncle Rob!'

'We decided when we got married that it would be better for everyone if I called him Robert in future,' Laura put in inconsequentially.

'Convenient,' Liam drawled.

She shook her head. 'Why are you making this so hard for me, Liam?' she choked.

'"Hard for you"?' he repeated savagely. 'What I would really like to do is break your pretty little neck! I have no idea why you've come here, Laura.' He drew in a deeply controlling breath. 'I really think it might be better if you just left again.'

'Better for whom?' She was becoming angry herself now. 'Just what do you think happened eight years ago, Liam? Do you think I lied to Robert, tried to pass Bobby off as his son? Is that why you're so angry? Because I can assure you Robert was never in any doubt about the fact that he wasn't Bobby's father. He couldn't have been,' she added emotionally, her hands clenched tightly together.

Liam became very still, looking at her through narrowed lids. 'Why couldn't he?' he finally said slowly, obviously not seeing any of the answers in her face.

She turned in her seat, opening up her handbag. 'I brought a photograph of my own to show you, Liam.' She placed it in front of him, much the way he had done to her seconds ago.

Liam glanced down. 'I've already seen it, thanks,' he said, pushing away the photograph he had looked at so intently at the house a short time ago.

She nodded. 'What you can't see, what you can't possibly know, is that slightly out of this picture is a wheelchair. Robert's wheelchair,' she explained shakily. 'The wheelchair he had been confined to for twenty years.'

Liam reached out to slowly pull the photograph back towards him, peering down at the images.

Laura knew exactly what he would see on closer inspection; the way Robert's legs were bent slightly unnaturally, his awkwardness as he held baby Bobby in his arms. Robert had injured his lower spine playing rugby twenty years earlier, had been completely paralysed from the waist down.

'It never stopped him from doing the things he wanted to do.' Laura spoke tearfully. 'He was very supportive while I was pregnant, was present at the birth, would get up in the night and feed Bobby. He played with him for hours, never tired of being with him. Just looking at him…' she recalled brokenly. 'He cried the first time Bobby called him Daddy. He never believed he would be lucky enough to become a father, you see.'

Liam swallowed convulsively, looking down at the photograph once again. 'Were you in love with him?' he asked gruffly. 'Tell me, Laura!' he insisted harshly as she hesitated.

'I've tried to tell you how I felt about him, but you don't seem to be listening.' She sighed. 'I loved Robert very much. But I wasn't *in* love with him.' How could she have been, when the only man she had ever loved was sitting opposite her?

Was she getting through to him? Did Liam understand? Could he see—?

Liam straightened. 'I don't think this is the place for us to discuss this, Laura,' he said abruptly, pushing the glass of whisky away untouched.

'Will you come up to my suite with me?' He looked across at her with narrowed eyes.

He no longer looked dangerous, just weighed down with a sadness Laura didn't completely understand. But she would like to…

'Yes, I'll come with you,' she answered softly, picking her bag up in readiness for leaving.

Liam took a light hold of her elbow as they walked across the reception area to the lift, but the two of them moved apart once they had stepped inside, neither of them speaking.

Laura's tension started to rise again. So much depended on this conversation. So very much!

'Very nice,' she murmured dismissively once they were in the luxurious comfort of the sitting room in his suite.

Liam moved to the mini-bar, taking out a small bottle of whisky to pour the contents into a glass tumbler. 'For you,' he offered dryly, holding the glass out to her as she looked at him warily. 'You look as if you need it!'

She didn't like whisky, had never liked strong alcohol, but Liam was right; at the moment she felt in need of it! The first sip made her wince initially, but it was quickly followed by a warming sensation, seeming to settle those quivering butterflies in her stomach too.

'Let's sit down,' Liam suggested gently. 'At least, you sit down,' he amended once she had done exactly that. 'I think better standing on my feet,' he acknowledged ruefully.

Laura wasn't sure she wanted him to be able to think better; she would rather he just listened.

'I realise you haven't yet told me all you feel you want to,' Liam said softly. 'But maybe it will help if I first tell you a few things about my version of what happened eight years ago. What do you think?'

She thought that at the moment she was coward enough

to welcome putting off her own version if that was what Liam wanted her to do!'

'Go ahead,' she assented, taking another sip of the whisky. It really was quite relaxing.

Liam drew in a ragged breath. 'Well, I've already explained what I thought of you and your emotions eight years ago. What I haven't told you is that I—Laura, eight years ago I was in love with you! One hundred per cent completely in love with you!' he stated evenly.

Laura stared at him. He hadn't— He didn't— He couldn't have been!

Liam took in her dumbfounded expression. 'Sometimes, still, your emotions are so transparent,' he said. 'I was in love with you, Laura,' he repeated firmly. 'But, as I've already explained, I was ten years older than you, felt you had a lot of growing up, a lot of living still to do, before it would be fair for any man to ask you to devote your life just to him.' His expression was grim now.

Laura moistened dry lips. 'You said, when we met again last week, that you wished I had been this Laura eight years ago…' she remembered slowly, that remark perhaps starting to make more sense to her now.

Perhaps…

She gave a firm shake of her head. 'You couldn't have loved me eight years ago, Liam,' she said. 'You could never have left me in the way that you did if that had been the case. Certainly never have married someone else within weeks of leaving England. And me,' she added painfully.

He gave a heavy sigh. 'After that night, when we made love, I knew I had to get out of your life, give you chance to grow up without my influence. I didn't go straight to America when I left England; I went home to Ireland first. Perhaps you remember my telling you earlier today that my mother isn't yet aware that you're the same Laura from eight years ago…? I talked to her about you then,' he continued at her affirmative nod. 'Told her everything—'

'Everything?' Laura echoed.

'Everything,' Liam repeated. 'My mother agreed with me that your parents' death must have been a terrible blow for you, that you were bound to still be emotionally immature, that my making a clean break from your life was probably for the best—'

'I wasn't too immature to become a mother!' Laura reminded him tautly. 'Don't you think that you—and your mother—should have let me be the one to decide whether or not I was mature enough to know my own mind?' she demanded impatiently. 'And heart,' she added huskily.

'I always intended to come back, Laura,' Liam told her gruffly. 'It was never meant to be for ever.'

She looked up at him disbelievingly. 'You married someone else, Liam,' she reminded him.

'I missed you so much when I got to America, Laura. Drank too much,' he stated flatly. 'Sometimes I would lose days at a time,' he remembered. 'I'm making no excuses,' he assured at her sceptical expression. 'Diana was beautiful, obviously willing. I—It only happened the once. A few weeks later she told me she was pregnant. What can I say? I married her. Only to discover within weeks of the marriage that she had apparently made a mistake, that she wasn't pregnant, after all. It's the oldest trick in the book.' He groaned. 'And I fell for it!'

How ironic. How utterly, awfully ironic! Because back in England Laura had been genuinely pregnant with Liam's child.

Her expression hardened. 'What do you want me to say, Liam?'

'About my marriage?' He shrugged. 'Nothing. It's a mistake that I have to live with. But it was also a mistake that made it impossible for me to come back here to you. I knew you would never forgive me for marrying someone else, never believe that it was you I loved the whole time. But when I saw you again last week—!'

Laura had tensed, staring at him intently. 'What did you think then, Liam? How did you feel?'

'Initially? Stunned. Quickly followed by euphoria; I thought I was being given a second chance! But then you told me you were someone else's wife!' He shook his head. 'Seven years ago, after my divorce, I had no right to come back and tell you how I felt about you; the fact that you were married to someone else would have made the whole thing impossible. But then I found out you were a widow, that your husband had been over thirty years older than you—'

'You believed I had married Robert for his money,' Laura recalled dryly.

'I couldn't think of any other reason why— The age gap seemed too vast for it to be a love-match. The man was almost twenty years older than me, for goodness' sake! Then, at first, when I saw Bobby and realised—I had to rethink it all. I thought perhaps you had married Robert Shipley to give the child a name,' he admitted raggedly. 'At least, I began to hope that was what you had done. And then today I learnt that Robert had been your Uncle Rob. The man you had obviously adored eight years ago.'

'Of course I adored him,' she confirmed emotionally. 'He picked me up and put me back on my feet again when my parents died, was always there for me. Always!' she added shakily, remembering all too vividly her own euphoria, quickly followed by heartbreak on learning of Liam's marriage to another woman, when she had discovered she was expecting Liam's child. Robert had cared for her. 'But I wasn't in love with him, Liam. Nor he with me. Our marriage was that of two very good friends, each caring deeply for the other, joined together by the love we both had for an innocent child.'

'How you must have hated me all these years.' Liam looked ashamed.

'Yes.' She wasn't about to lie to him; she *had* hated him—for leaving her, for marrying someone else, for not being there when their son was born. 'For a while I did,' she agreed. 'Until Bobby was born, probably. There was too much love in my heart then to feel hatred for anybody.' Least of all, she realised now, the man who had given her Bobby, given *Robert* Bobby.

'I love him, too, you know,' Liam told her huskily.

'I know you do.' She nodded understandingly. 'At first, when I realised I was pregnant, I didn't know what to do. It was Robert who said I had to tell you. He was even willing to go to America with me so I could tell you. He hated all the fuss that was made when he had to fly anywhere,' she recalled affectionately. 'But he was willing to do it to help me find you. Then we saw the photographs of your wedding in the newspapers,' she said bleakly.

'Oh, Laura…!'

'No.' She put up a shaky hand to stop Liam as he would have come down on his haunches beside her chair. 'It all has to be said, Liam,' she told him flatly. 'The truth told at last.' She drew in a ragged breath. 'I was twenty-one years old, in my last year of a university degree, and pregnant—and the father of my baby had just married someone else! Robert knew that I—I wanted to keep my baby. He—he offered to marry me, to take care of both me and the baby. Now we come to the difficult bit, Liam.' She looked up at him with tear-wet eyes.

He squeezed her hand. 'If it's any consolation, Laura, I know I deserve whatever you're going to say next.'

She stood up, putting down the glass of whisky she had only sipped at. 'It isn't a question of deserving anything, Liam,' she told him. 'If I had been different eight years ago, perhaps none of this would have happened. But the fact of the matter is we are both who we are, what we are. And if you had asked me to marry you eight years ago, Liam, then I would have said yes.' She again answered the question he had once put to her. 'But, with hindsight, I—I have to say that I wouldn't change a single thing about what actually did happen the last eight years!'

His throat moved convulsively. 'Because you married the man you loved after all…?'

'Haven't you been listening to a single thing I've said, Liam?' she challenged impatiently, her expression one of exasperation now. 'I loved Robert; I wasn't *in* love with him. But…' She paused, drawing in a deep breath. 'I have to be honest with you, Liam, and tell you that I can't regret my marriage to him. He was a wonderful husband and father; neither Bobby or I could have had better.' There, she had said it!

Because it had to be said. If there were to be any future relationship at all between Liam and herself, even that of friendship just for Bobby's sake, then Liam had to understand she regretted making none of the choices that had been open to her, that she would never have a denigrating word said about Robert, on any subject, within her hearing.

She hadn't been in love with Robert, but she had loved him deeply, and she knew that Bobby felt the same about the man he had known as his daddy. How Liam, with the knowledge that he was Bobby's biological father, intended dealing with that she had no idea. But he would have to deal with it in a way that was acceptable to her. Otherwise she would fight all the way any claim he tried to make on Bobby. She owed Robert that, at least.

Liam looked across at her with narrowed, thoughtful eyes. 'You asked me a short time ago why I hadn't told you that I knew I was Bobby's real father,' he began slowly. 'My answer was I was waiting for you to tell me. But there's a lot more to it than that, Laura,' he continued firmly as she would have spoken. 'Being a father isn't about impregnating a woman. It's being there for her during the sometimes scary days of pregnancy, being at her side during the birth, helping to care for and nurture the child once it's born. All the things that Robert did, in fact,' he acknowledged. 'The deep affection you had for him once frightened the hell out of me—eight years ago I thought you felt more for him than you did for me! But it doesn't frighten me any more, Laura. Now I'm just grateful to him. For being there for you, and Bobby, when I couldn't be or simply wasn't,' he admitted sadly.

The tears were swimming in Laura's eyes now. 'Do you really mean all that?' she breathed.

'Of course I mean it,' he replied. 'I'm not expecting to just walk into Bobby's life, announce that I'm his real father and take over that role as if it's my right! Because it isn't. I have to earn that right. In the same way I have to earn the right to tell you I'm still in love with you,' he carried on. 'That I've never stopped being in love with you,' he added emotionally.

'Oh, Liam…!' she choked tearfully.

'Is that, Oh, Liam, you'll never be able to convince me of that?' he asked. 'Or is it, Oh, Liam, I'll let you try if it's what you really want to do?' He looked at her with narrowed eyes.

Laura drew in a deep breath; it was now or never! 'It's, Oh, Liam, I do love you,' she admitted shyly, holding her breath as she waited for his response.

He became very still, eyeing her warily. 'Is that, I love you, Liam, or is that, I'm *in* love with you, Liam?'

She gave a shaky laugh. 'Which do you think?'

He raised his eyes heavenwards. 'After the confusion of the last week—I have no idea!' he admitted. 'Although I'm hoping it's the latter,' he added. 'You have no idea how much I'm hoping that!'

Oh, she thought she did—if it was anything like the way she felt!

'I love you very much, Laura. I've never stopped being in love with you,' he assured her. 'And, if you'll give me the chance, I would like the time to convince you of that.'

She took a step towards him. 'Don't you think we've wasted enough time already?' She took another step.

Liam covered the short distance that was left between them, sweeping her into his arms, holding her so tightly against him he was in danger of snapping her in half. 'I love you, Laura! I love you so much it hurts!' He groaned into the softness of her throat. 'I never want to be without you again!'

She could feel him shaking as she put her own arms about his waist and held him just as tightly as he was holding her. 'You won't be,' she promised. 'Not ever again!'

As his mouth claimed possession of hers, lips moving passionately against her, sipping, tasting, Liam desperate to make her a part of him, Laura knew that this time they wouldn't be parted by anything, or anyone.

This time it was for ever…

EPILOGUE

'OH, LOOK how tiny she is.' Bobby glanced up excitedly at Liam as they stood side by side looking down into the tiny hospital crib. 'Isn't Hannah beautiful?'

Liam glanced at Laura as she lay in the hospital bed, the two of them sharing a smile of complete love as Bobby enthused about his hours-old baby sister, Hannah Mary.

'Gorgeous. But not as beautiful as your mother,' Liam answered Bobby huskily, raising Laura's hand up to his mouth as he kissed the softness of her skin. 'Thank you,' he mouthed silently.

'When can we take her home, Mummy?' Bobby pressed excitedly.

Laura smiled at her beloved son, so pleased that he had taken this new addition to their family so well.

She and Liam had been married for a year now—a year of complete happiness, but also of necessary adjustments for all of them. Bobby most of all. He had had to learn to share his mother with 'Uncle Liam'. Now he had to share her with a baby sister too…

'Tomorrow, probably,' she answered sleepily. The labour with Hannah had been much shorter than with Bobby, but very tiring.

Liam had been with her this time, every day of her pregnancy, all through the hours of labour. As she had no doubts he would be with her every day for the rest of her life.

During Laura's maternity leave Perry was in charge of Shipley Publishing. Liam's book had been published three months ago, had been at the top of the bestseller list for two of those, and was looking likely to remain there for some time.

Laura knew she had never been so happy, knowing herself completely loved, and completely in love with Liam in return. And now they had a daughter as well as a son.

Liam had told her at the outset of their marriage that he thought Bobby should continue to think of him as 'Uncle Liam', in the hope that one day Bobby would decide to call him Daddy, simply because he wanted to. Telling Bobby the whole truth about his birth, they had decided together, could wait until he was older.

'Can I hold her?' Bobby asked softly. 'Can I, Mummy?'

Laura smiled. 'If you sit in this chair next to the bed I'm sure Dad—er, Uncle Liam will pick her up and give her to you.' She blushed slightly at the slip she had just made.

But it was how she always thought of Liam now. He had become Bobby's father, loved him, played with him, scolded him slightly if it were necessary, listened to him. Everything a father should do. And she knew if Robert could see them all now that he would be happy that Bobby and Laura had someone who loved them both so deeply.

'Will you, Daddy?' Bobby looked up almost shyly at Liam. 'Please?'

Laura watched as Liam swallowed the lump in his throat, her own eyes swimming with tears. It was the first time Bobby had called him Daddy…

But as she watched Bobby cuddling Hannah, Liam bending solicitously over both of them, Laura knew it wouldn't be the last time.

They were a real family now.

Complete.